THREE DEATHS

THREE DEATHS

by Josip Novakovich

SNARE

Edited by John Goldbach
Designed by Chris Tucker
Copyedited by Ann Ward
Typeset in Sabon and Albertus

Library and Archives Canada Cataloguing in Publication

Novakovich, Josip
       Three deaths / Josip Novakovich.
Poems.
ISBN 978-0-9865765-1-5
       I. Title.

PS3564.O925T47 2010   813'.54   C2010-905185-8

Printed and bound in Canada
Represented in Canada by the Literary Press Group
Distributed by LitDistCo
SNARE BOOKS
4832 A Avenue Du Parc
Montreal QC
H2V 4E6
snarebooks.wordpress.com

Canada Council   Conseil des Arts
for the Arts   du Canada

Snare Books gratefully acknowledges the financial support of the
Canada Council for the Arts.

TABLE OF CONTENTS

To all the living Novakovićes: Živili!

BE PATIENT

Year: 1952

Place: Daruvar, Socialist Republic of Croatia, Socialist Federal Republic of Yugoslavia

Doctor Marić held up the injection with a thin needle, which gleamed in the beam of the morning sun; he held it up as though aiming for the sky and said, This is a wonderful thing. It won't hurt at all, and it will prevent your children from getting the measles.

They stick a needle into you? asked Lyerka. I'm scared of needles.

It won't hurt at all, Nenad, her father, replied.

How do you know?

I've had lots of those when I was sick.

A boy in front of them cried.

So why is he crying?

From fear, not pain, explained the doctor.

I won't cry, she said.

When the doctor pushed in the needle, Lyerka's dark brown eyes grew wet, but she didn't let out a sound. A couple of brilliant tears rolled down her long eyelashes.

Now, that's my girl, said Nenad.

A nurse rubbed alcohol over the puncture, and covered it with gauze, and said, Hold it there for a while.

Lyerka did. A scarlet spot of blood appeared on the gauze.

You have a beautiful girl, the nurse said to Nenad.

I know. I don't know what I did to deserve such beauty.

Oh, you know what you did! We all deserve beauty, but few of us get it.

You have nothing to complain of.

Nenad noticed her deft long fingers, and he admired her blond hair, curving forward over her ears. It wasn't real blond, but chemical, yet it looked natural, complementing her dark blue eyes.

Oh, thank you! It's so rare in socialism to get a compliment. It's a bourgeois manner.

Life is too sad not to indulge in little pleasantries, he retorted.

Heading out the door, Nenad paused to check out the nurse's form as she leaned over to put the needle into a candle flame—very thin waist and wide hips.

Tata, have you forgotten something? asked Lyerka.

No.

Why is she burning the needle? So it will hurt more?

So nobody will get sick. Fire kills the germs.

He held Lyerka's hand and admired how small it was in his big fist. His hand had been enlarged through too much work and appetite, which he'd inherited from his father, who had basically eaten himself to death. At least he managed to die before World War II. There was a blessing there, at least for him.

Lyerka skipped steps over the cobbles in the town centre, past a rusty hot water fountain, and they walked into an ice cream parlour. You took it so well, my sweetie, you deserve a little strawberry ice cream.

She licked it, sticking out her little red tongue, like a kitten licking milk.

How do you feel?

Good. It's nice to be taking a walk with you.

I know. I am usually too busy to do this, but I promise we'll do it every day.

Lyerka smiled wide. But no more needles, she said.

You didn't like it, of course. Does it still hurt?

No. It's fine. It just itches a little.

No worse than a bee sting?

Much better.

A stray dog, with long hanging ears, came up to Lyerka, and Lyerka petted him. The dog blinked and licked her hand.

See, he loves me.

He loves the ice cream sticking to your fingers. But yes, he loves you; everybody does.

She lifted one of his hanging ears and petted it.

Don't touch him. He could have all sorts of diseases.

Could we take him home?

No. Where would he stay?

You could build him a doghouse. It's easy for you; you can build anything.

Nenad laughed. Yes, a doghouse I could, but I don't see why. Plus, the dog is bigger than you. What if he has rabies? He could bite you.

He won't. He likes me. Look at him.

She buried her little fingers in the dog's long orange hairs.

Nenad pulled her by the hand, away from the dog.

Uh, that hurts, Daddy! That's my sore arm.

I didn't know it was sore. Sorry, we have to get home.

She didn't say anything. The dog followed a few paces behind. She turned around. He wants to come with us. Look at those big eyes! He is crying.

Dogs can't cry.

The dog furrowed his brows, and there were creases on his forehead; he looked worried and thoughtful.

Don't look at him, Nenad said. That encourages him.

But why can't I have a dog?

We have enough cats running around our yard.

They are all wild, and I can't pet them.

At least you learned that lesson when that nasty tomcat nearly scratched your eye out.

Oh, he was just scared. He's nice now that I bring out some leftovers.

I didn't know we had leftovers.

At home, Marta had just brought in a pile of scrap wood in a pleated basket from the workshop.

You all look ruddy and fresh, she said.

The walk did us good. The sun is strong, and the wind from the mountains is chilly. And to talk with Lyerka means happiness, you know.

There's a letter for you, from the taxation office. She pointed to a blue envelope with a stamp. Nenad checked out the stamp: the walled city of Dubrovnik. He used to collect stamps.

Why are you staring at the envelope? The letter is inside; won't you read it? They want you to pay more taxes.

Of course, when did they want me to pay less? Bastards, they won't let a decent man live.

I suppose they are just doing their job. You don't want to end up in jail, do you?

I'm not afraid of their jails. I've been to worse places in the war. Now, of course I'll go pay, but how am I going to feed our growing family?

We are doing fine, praise the Lord.

Yes, the Lord and me.

Are you all hungry?

Marta, a solid woman with a thin nose and small green eyes beneath a tall forehead, cooked pancakes, *pala inke*, for supper. She put cottage cheese with a bit of sugar inside the pancakes and offered them to their children. Pretty soon there was a measured triple knock on the thick oak door, and Nenad's stocky brother Drago (endowed with emphatically upturned black eyebrows) came in with his sensationally pale and nearly translucent wife, Maria. There was no phone in the entire town, and if people wanted to visit, they came directly over, risking being turned away if the family was busy, but after darkness gathered hardly anybody worked, although most of them fussed, canning and pickling peppers or dancing on their bleeding grapes or on sliced cabbage or reading old yellow-papered novels. Nobody had TV sets, and guests were in demand as a source of entertainment, so members of an extended family were rarely turned away.

Marta brought out tablecloths to adorn the otherwise naked aged wood. The pale beechwood resembled human flesh in hue, and to her it seemed indecent; it would have to be clad for the visitors. There were a few stains from duck-soup grease, and a burned spot from a brimming-hot frying pan off the stove, and a few scars from children's cutting with knives, and there were lots of knives all over the house and in the workshop, where Nenad made tables and chairs for a living.

Would you like some rose-hip tea? Marta offered. We also have some white wine. My husband no longer drinks anything alcoholic; his doctor tells him it's best not to.

Oh, doctors, Drago answered. They always tell you what not to do, but it would be better if they told you what to do. Yes, I'll have a glass of wine.

And so would I, said his blue-eyed wife, Maria. She was half

German, half Czech. After the last world war, her parents were driven out like many Germans, and that Maria could remain had to do with her being married to Drago, who had to his credit killing four ambushed German soldiers.

Drago drew a loud gulp of greenish wine, exceedingly sour and tart. Strange days—suddenly we can't talk about Mother Russia anymore, and America is our new friend.

Politics, they always change, it's best not to talk about it, Marta said.

Why not? Nenad said. You can't spend your life in fear that something bad will happen. A lot of bad stuff happened, and a lot more will, but we can at least talk about it.

We are getting all sorts of modern help from America, said Drago, better antibiotics, better radios, better beans. Can you believe it, Serbian beans, *pasulj*, for years came from America.

I know, and today our children were inoculated against the measles, Nenad said. Yugoslavia is the first country in the world to get the medicine!

That is strange, Maria said. Why don't they use it in America first?

They don't have a crisis like we do.

It's not a crisis, Drago said. You get it, and so what. A few spots, a fever.

Maybe you are thinking of rubella. This is rubeola. The high fevers can damage your heart.

Oh, everything can damage your heart. You don't brush your teeth right, or you sleep on the wrong side; you spend too much time in bed or too little; you work too hard or too little, and your heart fails.

Americans are nice to us, Marta said.

Well, the American friendship is all self-interest, Drago said. It's military propaganda to keep us away from the Soviet bloc.

I don't care about the motives as long as the deeds are good, said Nenad. Lyerka, apple of my eye, will you play a song for our guests?

Lyerka, dressed in white, glowed. She could pick a few melodies on the piano, and she improvised in the right key "Ave Maria." She stood in her tiny clogs next to the piano, dancing slowly while choosing the keys.

Beautiful, isn't she, said Marta, her mother. Upon hearing the compliment, Lyerka smiled, and her eyes seemed to grow in size. Dimples appeared on her flushed and round cheeks. The blackness of her hair transcended itself into flickers of blue.

She's smart too, said Marta. Ask her to multiply numbers, and see what happens.

What is seven times seven? asked Drago.

Almost fifty, she answered.

What do you mean by almost fifty?

Forty-nine.

And what is nine times nine?

Just a little over eighty.

Bravo! Maria said. And she is only five?

Almost five! answered Lyerka.

Marta took off her scarf, shook her curly hair, which sprang up, increasing in volume, and she gathered it and tied it into a tall bun. Her life was fulfilled. She had a clever and curious son, who wanted to become a journalist, and an older daughter, who liked to read the encyclopedia, and now she had a brilliant little girl, who would grow up to be a music teacher or even perhaps a doctor. In socialism women could study like men, and since they were not drunks you could foretell their future.

For the evening meal Marta prepared *zganci*, hot corn cereal, with fresh cow milk. Lyerka tiptoed to the stove, where a pot of boiled milk was cooling off and forming a wrinkled cover of cream. She scooped it up in a soup spoon, which in her tiny hand looked like a ladle. While Lyerka chewed the cream, looking beatific, Marta said, You should never walk barefoot; where are your clogs? You'll catch a cold!

Nenad said grace, and at the end of the meal he kissed everybody good-night. He was making sure they would have an orderly life, something he hadn't experienced in his upbringing, where his father, damaged by World War I and captivity in Russia, had a bad temper. He couldn't control his appetite because he had spent four years starving in Siberia. Every meal to him seemed to be the last one, so he devoured as much as possible, with lots of *feferoni*, yet he was thin, stringy, and fiery.

The following day, after a lunch consisting of bread, milk, and honey, Lyerka scratched her arm.

Nenad asked, It hurts?

Tata, it still itches.

But it doesn't hurt?

No. Could I have a glass of water? I am thirsty.

Can't you get it for yourself?

You are right, I am just a little tired.

Fine, I'll get you a glass. He poured the water from a bucket on a chair. They had no indoor plumbing; Marta had brought in a bucket drawn from their spindle-well.

Lyerka gulped the water greedily.

She's kind of red in the face, said Marta.

A bit flushed from the wind. She went out to look for the cats. The last gasp of winter, it's energizing.

Marta felt Lyerka's forehead. She's warm.

They say it's normal. After the shot, you can run a slight fever for three days.

Strange idea, to take healthy children to the hospital and give them fevers in the name of health.

That's good planning, and Americans are great at that. They've knocked out TB, and now they'll get rid of most diseases.

What are we going to die of then?

Old age.

I'm sleepy. Can I go to bed? asked Lyerka.

But it's the middle of the day, and you are too old for naptime.

She is not too old, Nenad said. Spaniards do it all their lives.

Marta said, We should give her some aspirin.

It's not fever, only a slight temperature rise, perfectly normal.

It would be normal to keep it down.

I think it's good for the body to learn how to fight off fevers. Probably the inoculation works better with the heat—the body is producing antibodies. It's like a little foundry. Foundries are always hot. Fire kills the germs. He closed his eyes and saw the needle in the flame held by deft, elongated fingers.

I'll give her at least some lemonade. Marta took out a lemon, sliced it in half, and squeezed it into a glass.

It's great that our country is making friends in Africa, Nenad said, so we can have lemons. How old were you when you had your first lemon? I had mine in 1935. We didn't know that there was a difference between lemons and yellow pears, so we ate the skins too and wondered how such a bitter and sour fruit could be so popular.

Thanks, Mama. My throat is dry and scratchy. Can I have more?

Marta felt Lyerka's forehead.

Jesus, you are burning up! Where is the thermometre? Nenad, come over here, she's all red.

She's shivering. My God, she is in trouble. Take her to the clinic right away!

Nenad tried to place her on the bicycle in the child-carrying seat, but she couldn't sit up straight.

She's too weak to sit up, and I don't think she has any sense of balance, he said. I better carry her.

As he walked up the cobbles on the hill, he sweated. Her heat was getting to him; he panted.

At the clinic the doctor on duty smoked a cigar and asked, Fever and you get excited? Children have fevers all the time. His moustache was grey and white, vertical white stripes, except under the nose, where they were yellow, black and yellow. But as he looked at Lyerka, he said, You are right, she looks too hot.

A black-haired nurse, who also had a moustache, put the thermometre under Lyerka's tongue. Lyerka's chin shook. The doctor felt her neck below her ears. Her glands are a little too swollen.

What is it? asked Nenad.

An allergic reaction to the inoculation. Probably nothing serious, but we have to drive her to the hospital right away. We have one more child with high fever and neck swelling like that, and they are already waiting for the car downstairs.

The ambulance drove over potholes in town and then over the mud and gravel to the hospital in Pakrac, twenty-two kilometres away. The ambulance thudded on the wooden bridge over the river Pakra. The hospital was painted all blue.

A father and his son, the same age as Lyerka, went through the doors first. The son was shivering violently, and he moaned more than Lyerka did.

Nenad and his daughter waited in a dark corridor.

Can't they turn on the lights? asked Nenad.

No, we have to save on electricity, said a cleaning woman dressed in dark blue and sweeping, raising the dust, which accumulated from crumbs of caked soil slipping out from underneath people's soles.

Lyerka moaned and then coughed.

Will you stop sweeping dust and germs right into our mouths?

No, I can't. A job is a job. It has to be done.

Do it when we are gone.

Most people are gone.

Don't you see the child is coughing?

It's a hospital. Everybody is coughing. What do you expect?

Get out of our way, you smart fat-ass!

Don't become abusive, comrade. Who do you think you are?

But when Nenad stood up and swore colourfully (*Jebo te vrag!*), red in the face, she turned her back and swept at the other end of the corridor.

The sound of children's crying was emerging from a couple of rooms. And farther down the corridor an old man was wailing, Mama! He was calling through the ages, from perhaps his ninetieth year to the middle of the previous century, for a time when he was a helpless toddler with a voluptuous mother, who by now was probably dust and bones in the ground in one of the rickety cemeteries in the hills. On his deathbed, and nobody attended to him. The cries stopped and there was a long moan, which trailed off and became a wet wheeze, assuming a ghostly echo from cavernous lungs.

Lyerka leaned her face against her father's arm, against the scratchy herringbone-patterned wool of his jacket. He put his hand on her head and petted her hair over her ear.

Daddy, can we just go home? It's better there.

But you need help. They have good doctors here.

What do good doctors do?

They make you healthy. Were they good? he wondered. They always behaved like they were; they boasted of their Zagreb Medical School education, which they said was the same thing as Viennese education, maybe even better because they adhered to the old standards of enforcing a huge repertoire of memorization.

He stood up and knocked on the off-white door, and as he knocked some of the cracked paint crumbled and fell on the floor.

Comrade, not so violently! You are making a mess, said the cleaning woman. I'll have to sweep again.

Just you dare!

He knocked again and then opened the door.

A doctor was combing his hair in front of a mirror, and a nurse was putting lipstick on her wide mouth.

Don't you see we are taking a break?

I see, but my child is terribly ill and we've been waiting. I never saw Comrade Vedri and his son come out.

They didn't. They are in the other room. We've been working since six this morning. Fine, bring her in.

The nurse shook a thermometre, snapping her wrist thrice, and opened the child's mouth to put it in. Lyerka's teeth chattered. She bit the thermometre hard as her jaw clenched it.

Oh, my, don't bite through that glass, said the nurse.

After a minute, she pulled out the thermometre and held it

up against the bald light bulb. It's forty-three degrees. That is way too high; she'll need a lot of aspirin and a cold press.

Well, give it to her then, said Nenad.

Of course, we know what to do. The nurse got an aspirin, 500 mg., and put it on a spoon.

Daddy, the puppy is hungry, Lyerka said. Promise to feed him.

Yes, I'll feed him, don't worry.

Comrade, said the doctor, who do you think will win in the semis, Dinamo or Hajduk? Tito is rooting for Hajduk, and so am I.

I could care less. Just help her.

I know. I need to keep some kind of conversation going to keep us sane, to keep you from worrying too much.

Should I worry?

No, but we'll wait a little to see how she responds. Open your mouth!

They put the spoon with aspirin on her tongue, and then poured water from a glass into her mouth. The water spilled over. Lyerka coughed, and the aspirin flew out of her mouth like a little white dove out of a church window. The pill fell onto the checkered floor and rolled around, disappearing under the cupboard.

Why are you spitting it out, darling? asked the nurse.

She can't help it, Nenad said. It's a reflex.

Let me see. The doctor shone a thin flashlight into Lyerka's throat, pressing down on her tongue with the handle of an aluminum spoon.

Hmm, her throat is too swollen and red; she won't be able to swallow such a large tablet. Fine, we'll crush the aspirin so she can drink it.

Lyerka gulped the water loudly and spat it out. It's yucky!

You want more sugar, less sugar?

More.

The doctor read the sports pages. Nenad rolled the brim of his hat.

After fifteen minutes they measured her temperature again.

She's not responding yet. She'll need more time and a cold press and an IV and more aspirin. We'll have to keep her overnight, just like that boy.

Should I stay here?

It's better if you go home and come back tomorrow morning. Nervous parents don't help; they make us nervous.

Daddy, don't leave, Lyerka said.

I'll be right back, and I'll bring you some ice cream.

She smiled and closed her eyes.

The ambulance drove the two fathers home. Vedri pulled out a bottle of greenish slivovitz and swallowed two loud gulps. My throat is too dry from all this anxiety, he explained. Would you like a shot?

No, I don't drink.

I don't know how you can stand it to be sober in a situation like this. What is going on? Do you understand?

Who does?

Nenad and Marta could not sleep that night.

It's my fault, Marta said.

What do you mean, your fault?

I was too happy and proud with how beautiful she was.

What do you mean, was. Is. She is.

I know, but what if she …

Don't say it.

The other two children, a boy and a girl, slept.

How about if we pray? he suggested.

It's that bad? I knew it.

Prayer is a good idea anyway.

He got out of bed and played the guitar, slowly, a church song.

When will you pray then? Marta asked.

God loves music more than our voices.

How do you know that?

My soul knows that.

Early in the morning, before any redness showed in the paling sky, Nenad bicycled to the hospital. The little dynamo hummed against the tire and produced enough light to illuminate the unpredictable road ahead. There were a couple of hills too steep for the bicycle, and he walked up them and sweated despite the cold wind. Lonesome dogs were howling at one another from two remote hills.

He found a different doctor, who looked strikingly similar to the night-shift doctor, except his hair was silvery; it looked as though the same doctor had aged a decade overnight, but it was definitely a different doctor, shorter and thinner, standing irresolutely with a couple of plump nurses in the emergency room.

How is she doing? Nenad asked.

Who? We have lots of girls on the ward. There's some kind of epidemic.

My daughter, Lyerka Vukov.

Oh, yes, we can't get her fever down. It's still forty-three. And of course, with such a long fever, she's delirious.

So, will she make it?

Let's hope so.

Of course, I hope. Can you do something more than hope?

I hope so.

Are you joking or something?

We'll put her on IVs again so she doesn't dehydrate, and with more liquids in her body, she could cool down.

Can I see her?

She was red and her lips were green, and she mumbled about a puppy.

Sweetie, I will get you the puppy. He's waiting for you.

Lyerka grasped his thumb, giving it a hot squeeze. But she had no strength to do it for more than a few seconds, and her hand dropped and she continued to moan. Her neck was swollen, bigger than before.

What did she eat before she got sick? asked the doctor. Maybe she ate some poisonous mushrooms?

Not this time of the year—nothing's growing in the winter, other than oyster mushrooms, and those are never poisonous.

Dry mushrooms? Old pork?

We don't eat pork.

You are Jews? Adventists?

Neither, but we just don't. The problem is, she's had an inoculation against rubeola. What do you think is the problem?

I don't know, an allergic reaction. We'll give them some milk.

Milk?

Yes, milk helps with allergies and poisons.

She had plenty of milk. You have nothing stronger? No real medication against this?

We'll think about it. Just let me think.

Well, think fast. If you save her, I'll give you ten thousand dinars.

Lyerka gasped and breathed fast like a dog after a long run. Her mouth was open, and her little red tongue trembled.

And I'll sign over my forest to you, Nenad said.

I'll do what I can.

His nurse had placed wet towels over her body. They gave her an IV.

Nenad waited in the corridor, which was filthy with muddy print marks of boots of all sizes, in all directions. Clearly, people here walked in circles, disoriented and frantic as they waited, and so did he, with his hat brim rolled in his left hand and his right hand scratching a sore spot on his scalp, layered with dandruff, until it bled.

The fever is going down, just a little, but it's in the right direction, said the doctor. Don't panic. We'll do all we can, and we are talking to the specialists in Zagreb over the phone.

Nenad wondered whether the sudden activity by the doctor had anything to do with the offered money. The motives didn't matter; saving his *chedo*, his dear child, did.

So the thing to do was to go home and raise the money. He bicycled back, first to Drago to ask him for a thousand dinars, which Drago gave him without comment. He rode home and collected his savings hidden in the attic under a pile of red roof tiles. He gathered ten thousand, a small fortune. With that he had planned to buy a new Opel or perhaps a Mercedes. So much for that. He bicycled back to the hospital. In a curve the bike slid over gravel, and he fell, banging his elbow like a child.

He took the same doctor aside, onto the muddied, spotted-marble floor of the dark corridor, near white-painted windows, and said, Doctor, how is she doing? He felt unsteady, and as he leaned against the window frame, thick cracked lead paint crumbled and peeled off in little sheets.

To be frank, the fever has come back, and we can't knock it down.

What is it?

It could be meningitis, as a side effect. Apparently there's a lot of it around.

You call it a side effect? It sounds pretty major.

Well, we don't know. We actually don't have the blood-test results yet.

What are you waiting for? I'm giving you ten thousand dinars, that's what a factory worker would make in two years, to save her. You have to try harder.

It's not necessary; I'll do my best. But contrary to what he was saying, he stretched out his hand and took the blue envelope, with the stamp of the walls of Dubrovnik, and placed it in the right front pocket of his pants, keeping his hand in the pocket, deep, as though he was shifting his balls into a more comfortable position.

You promise you'll watch her? Consult your best books and other doctors. Maybe there are American doctors in Belgrade at the embassy who would know about these side effects? Can you call them?

Yes, we'll call them. I'll do what I can. Let me go now—talking with you won't help her. We'll try a few things.

May I go with you?

Better not at the moment. Just wait here, and we'll call you in.

Nenad paced up and down the corridor on the spotted black and yellow floor. The light of the thinly clouded day spread through white curtains and bounced off the floor in a jaundiced hue. What to think in a situation like this? He'd been under the gun several times in the war, and it felt simpler—immediate fear, possibility of a clean and violent end. He'd even had shrapnel lodged near his kidney, but two years after the war, it crawled out of him, and he woke up with a small wound bleeding calmly. The shrapnel looked like somebody's iron molar. He'd much rather be hit with shrapnel again. The mix of hope and fear only increased his dread.

He was not the only one pacing—there were four other parents. They all smoked. Nenad knelt near a bench and prayed. God, if you save my daughter, I will serve you and do whatever you want me to do. I will give biblical names to all my children. I will witness for you and go to jail if necessary. And if you don't save her, I will become a communist. Not that I am in a position to make threats, but isn't it a good idea to make friends in this godless country?

Before he could say amen, he heard a scream.

He stood up. A doctor was speaking softly to a mother and holding her shoulder.

What, he is dead?

Yes, two children are dead.

How about my child? asked Nenad.

Is Dara all right? cried a woman next to him.

Wait, not so fast. We'll give you the names.

Is Lyerka alive?

Nenad hoped it would be another child, not his.

Dara is dead, said the doctor. Sorry to say.

Are you sure? Maybe she just passed out.

What can I tell you? This is a major tragedy.

You couldn't do anything?

And Lyerka?

Alive, we are working on her.

Nenad kneeled against the wall and prayed on.

Look at him, his child is alive, and he is praying to God, said a man. And he has money. I am sure he paid them.

That's how it goes—the world always favors those with money.

Maybe we should have prayed to God.

He has probably given money to his God too.

The two dead children were wheeled away, covered with white sheets; one had her eyes wide open, and the other had them closed, and on his eyelids were placed two sugar cubes to keep the eyes closed and to decrease the bitterness of death.

A few minutes later Nenad knocked on the door of the room with four beds.

The doctor and the nurse were playing cards at a table. Next to them was a large red apple on an orange-coloured plate.

Is she alive?

Yes, she must be.

Nenad ran to the white bedside. Lyerka moved her face toward him and smiled. Her eyes gleamed; she looked radiant. Her hair emitted indigo-blue rays, or so it seemed to his wet eyes, refracting the light and intensifying it, as though he were sinking into the dark of an ocean and looking upward toward the glare of the unreachable sunshine.

Nenad leaned over and kissed her forehead. It was astonishingly hot.

Can't you give her more aspirin?

Oh, she's had plenty. She's running about forty-one. It's not all that bad. It used to be worse. It's going down, sort of.

You think she will make it?

She might, she might.

Is there nothing else you can do for her?

No, we just have to wait now, like you.

And so you play cards?

And so we play cards. Health is a game of luck like cards. At this point we can only hope to be lucky.

He walked back to Lyerka. Her mouth was twisted, and her eyes were glazed. Foam floated down her cheek. Look at me! he said. But her eyes seemed to be looking beyond him, through the walls, into the clouds, reflecting the clouds, becoming grey.

He had wasted her last minute of consciousness talking with the card-playing doctors. But maybe she hadn't been conscious in a while anyway.

Don't you see, she's dying, he said. Can't you do something? Oh?

Nenad looked into her eyes. They were hazing up, losing focus. A milkish hue covered the brown of her iris.

We did what we could. Many children died from this inoculation. They gave us a dosage that was way too strong.

Are you sure you did what you could? Maybe you gave up too soon? Isn't there some drug to keep the heart going?

They didn't reply but looked for the pulse in her neck.

He couldn't look at the cloudiness in her eyes, and he put his large hand over her face and pulled the eyelids down. They sprang back up, halfway.

Give me the apple, he said.

It was an old red apple from the late fall, with creased skin.

He sliced it and put two moon-shaped slices over her eyelids to keep them closed. An apple was the first gift of God to man, so be it. Maybe the apple will help her see all the way back into paradise.

He held her in his arms. Her temperature was becoming normal.

Why did she die? Maybe I didn't believe enough. But the whole world is full of unbelievers, and many of them do fine.

At home, when he brought her in, the older kids shrieked in fright.

He laid her down on her bed.

The siblings stood on the side and stared. Is she asleep? Nada asked.

You could put it that way, said Nenad.

The mother turned ghastly pale and said, I knew it.

What do you mean, you knew it.

I am not surprised. We were happy, we were too happy, for the first time in our lives the last few weeks. And I was too proud. I boasted that evening how she could multiply. God has punished us. I shouldn't have bragged about what a beautiful child we had.

Why do you think it has anything to do with you? Just now I thought it was my fault, that I didn't believe enough. Why do you think it has anything to do with us? Maybe God wanted her in his heavenly choir? Maybe she's happier there?

She is not there. She's nowhere.

And now the funeral had to be arranged. There was no cash left in the house.

Go ask them to give it back to you, Marta said.

I can't ride to Pakrac now. It's too far away. I don't care, life is over. I am exhausted.

We still must bury her.

I don't know what we must do. Maybe we can just keep her in the bedroom, maybe she will wake up.

Well, we must bury her; there's no other way.

No, it's all over.

Life goes on.

It doesn't.

It was so beautiful while it lasted. God gave, God took away. America took away.

Nenad bought a black flag on credit. Marta sewed it onto a pole, and Nenad stuck it out of the roof through a space between two loosened tiles. Sunshine streaked through one window, projecting a parallelogram onto the warped wooden floor.

He went to the printing press office in the centre of the town, near the Hungarian Calvinist church. The press used to publish a weekly newspaper but now published only death notices and festival posters.

Darkness filled the house, unabated by the ceremony surrounding death. Rather than buy a coffin, Nenad built one and varnished it. Yes, she said he could build anything. How much nicer it would be if he were building a doghouse. Maybe if he'd let the dog come in, her happiness would have carried her through the poisoning?

Before going to bed, he went over to the table where Lyerka lay in state and kissed her cheeks, which were frightfully cold and rubbery. It was as though the real body had burned away and vanished into the clouds and what remained was a death mask made of some special mix of rubber, plastic, and bread dough. It seemed a peculiar chemical mix, such as only German and American technology was capable of producing. But that couldn't be—death and cold corpses existed even before. Yes, but this was an American death. Of course, my thoughts are all rubbish, futile spasms of strained nerves. Here she is, and the soul is still somewhere near her body or in her body. It couldn't have left so fast.

He drifted to sleep to the sound of two lonesome dogs howling at one another somewhere in the hills, and then woke with a start when a blinding light filled the room. But as he stood up the light diminished and lifted, flowing out the window. And he heard a voice: I have heard your prayers. Be patient.

How can I be patient?

There was no answer, and the light completely vanished. The night light—was it moonlight or starlight or ghost light?—receded into blackness.

Who are you talking to? asked Marta. What is it about being patient?

God has asked me to be patient.

Oh, Nenad, God doesn't talk to people.

Yes, I saw him, his back. He passed through our room and nearly blinded me. I saw only the light after him, not his face, of course.

What do you need to be patient about?

About Lyerka. We will see her again.

Yes, when we die. You plan to die now?

You are cynical even now? No, God will resurrect her.

Did God tell you that?

Not quite, but I am sure that's what he meant.

How can you be sure?

Don't provoke me now!

I am just asking a simple and reasonable question.

No, you want me to doubt again. Doubt is what got me, us, into trouble.

He started to shout.

Now, is that a way to behave at your child's wake?

You tell me. How is one supposed to behave? Is there a book of manners to explain that?

Many people visited and wept at the sight of the blue child in the tiny coffin. Her rich black hair, curly and wavy, adorned her face.

Schultz, the Baptist minister, came over and showed Nenad the article in the daily newspaper, *Vijesnik*. 81 Children Die of the New Vaccine in Slavonia.

That is not that many. What, ten thousand got the vaccination, and my child had to die, Nenad said.

Can we pray?

For her soul?

Yes.

All children go to heaven, Nenad said. They can't sin. Why pray?

We can pray for you and your wife.

Don't worry about us, we'll do fine. It's too early for her to go to heaven. Let's pray for her resurrection.

In a few minutes we will. But first I'd like to tell you something about the American system. There you can sue for medical errors. You should find out what company did this vaccination, and go to the American embassy and file a lawsuit. They do experiments like this in the countries without medical malpractice laws—in Africa, and here.

You think they'd let me into the embassy?

You should ask for at least ten thousand dollars.

Money won't bring her back to life. Money doesn't mean anything.

You have other children. You could afford a better, healthier house.

What, you are saying my house isn't good enough. It's filthy to you?

No, but it's a little dark and gloomy.

The world is dark and gloomy. It's the vale of tears.

So maybe it's not so terrible to think of your child now in heaven.

Jesus resurrected children. He resurrected himself. He stayed dead for three days.

Marta came over and said, Would you like some tea? Linden tea? It's good for the nerves.

I am going to my workshop, Nenad said.

There he cut poplar boards and framed a box with a little door and a slanted roof.

The minister and Marta came and watched him, labouring in his cloud of reddish sawdust, but he didn't notice them.

Who needs a doghouse? Marta asked.

You never know, Nenad answered. It's good to be ready.

Later a procession was formed, and the casket was placed on a horse-drawn hearse. On the side of it several wreaths were hung, with black ribbon and purple writing expressing good wishes for Lyerka's afterlife. The parents and siblings followed immediately after the hearse, then uncles, aunts, and distant relatives, neighbours, acquaintances, and finally strangers, and lots of old women in black. The metal reinforcing the wooden wheels crunched the gravel in the streets. And on the side, not far from the coffin, limped a large orange dog with hanging ears and furrowed brows. He kept looking up at the coffin and squealing quietly. Can you chase him away? Marta said to Nenad.

No, he belongs here. He's our dog now.

We don't need a dog, she whispered.

Yes, we do.

APPLE

One snowless winter morning before going to school, I collected sawdust in baskets in Father's clog shop and dumped it out in the yard next to a walnut tree. The circular saw was running in his shop, yet I saw no father behind it. I found him in a corner, behind a pile of wooden soles, prostrate, praying. I was terrified of his praying.

Late that evening as Father drank warm milk and chewed dark bread, he told our grandmother how he'd heard someone calling him—the way Samuel was called—and yet he could see nobody. It was an angel of God calling him to prayer. That afternoon he had also felt someone touch him on the shoulder, and when he had turned around there was nobody. An angel of God had been there to strengthen him.

Grandmother said that she was glad to hear it, and then she coughed. When she didn't cough, her bronchial wheezing had a soothing rhythm to it, and I listened to it more than my father's stories, which went on all evening.

The next morning, Father walked around the town and begged everybody for forgiveness "in the name of Christ" for all the wrongs that he had wittingly and unwittingly committed. He gave his former assistant, who now had his own shop, two bales of ox-hide. Earlier my father had sold him a rotten bale, creating a bad reputation for the assistant's new business.

Father brought home an astonished old peasant, forcing him to take a large sum of money because, several years before, Father had forced the peasant to sell him wood too cheaply—the peasant had wept, to no avail, that he and his children could not make it through the winter on so little money.

The following Sunday, even though it was my father preaching in our Baptist church, I was bored, and made deep creases between the grains of the soft bench wood with my thumbnails, each crease representing one year—that's how long it seemed that the sermon lasted. Stealthily, I read a chapter from *A Journey to the Center of the Earth*, which I had stored in the Bible. A retired electrician and distant relative, who sat behind me, tapped me on my shoulder to make me stop. My father preached Christ's giving up His ghost on the cross, and in the middle of the sermon he wept.

Father had played the bass in the church orchestra and sang with the deepest voice in the choir. When he shouted at home, the whole household, including the cat, ran out into the yard. When he missed shaving for just one day, his chin was black; he often rubbed his raspy cheeks against mine, laughing—if he had pressed harder, he would have swept off my skin. The same man now cried in front of more than a hundred people. I blushed.

But at home, as if aware that I was ashamed of him, he said to me, "If you understood God's grace, you would have to weep." He took me out into the moonless night, and from the apple-scented garden he pointed to the stars swimming in moist, dizzying blackness. "See, God created the stars. It takes millions of years for the light to reach our eyes, and God's thought is everywhere in no time at all. God's thoughts are right here with us."

"I can't feel it," I said.

"You are lucky you can't. Moses could see God's radiance only from behind as It passed. We would die if we saw nearly as much. You cannot be close to God and live!"

It was January 6th, and snow stormed outside, slantedly. When I looked through the window, I had the feeling that the household floated into heaven sideways. The big patches of snow resembled the down of a huge, slain celestial bird, whose one wing covered the whole valley, and the spasmodic wing must have been flapping, because it was windy. As soon as the snow touched the ground, it melted.

After a day in the clog-making shop, Father stepped into the living room, solemn and luminous. Ivo read comic books. Father said to him, "Don't blaspheme against God by reading trash. Why don't you read the Bible, or study math?"

"I don't feel like it," said Ivo.

The cat, who was sleeping on the roof of a large clay stove, stretched herself and blinked, her pupils contracting in vertical slits, coiled her tail as if scared Father would deliver her a blow, and jumped off the stove. Usually she rushed to sit in his lap. Now she sat on the Bible on the chair next to my bed and licked her paws, now and then looking at him mistrustfully.

"And you," he addressed me, "how can you allow this dirty animal to sit on the Bible?" As if to punctuate his question, the cat twisted her body and licked the root of her tail. I chased her off the sombre book. Mother's slow, heavy steps resounded in the corridor, against the cement, louder and louder. She walked in with a basketful of wood and, breathing heavily, knelt in front of the stove and stirred the thin ashen embers with her bare fingers in such a quick way that she did not burn herself. Her method of doing it always disturbed me.

"Sons, why do you let Mother carry the wood? Why don't you help her?"

We made no reply.

He addressed me, "Yozzo, bring me an apple from the attic."

I went to the attic over the creaky wooden steps, and the flashlight didn't work. I was scared of the dark. I knew the attic very well, so I found the apples and pressed them with my thumb to find a large one, neither hard nor soft, but crunchy. Taking the red apple with his large hand from mine, he said, "I didn't know we had such beautiful apples—you can surely choose! I hope you choose your wife so well, so you won't look at other women and sin in your heart. Hum, there's nothing more joyous in this life than the beauty of a woman."

My mother said, "That's no way to talk to a child!" He replied, "It is."

"Will I ever be able to speak in tongues?" I asked him. "He can do it"—I pointed at Ivo—"though he reads garbage!"

"Though I speak with the tongues of men and of angels, and have not charity, I am become as sounding brass, or a tinkling cymbal. And though I have the gifts of prophecy, and understand all mysteries ... and though I have all faith, so that I could remove mountains, and I have not charity, I am nothing. Don't worry about the tongues, son."

"But if I spoke in tongues, then I'd be sure to go to heaven."

"He who wants to save his life, will lose it, and he who loses it for my sake, will gain it. Don't worry about salvation."

He looked at me for a long time. Then he dug his teeth, some of them made of gold, into the apple, his grey moustache spreading like a brush on the red skin of the fruit while he was biting. Saliva collected in my mouth as if he had chewed a lemon. He ate one half slowly and left the rest on the plate. A haze of brown soon covered the white crystal apple meat. His face suddenly lost colour, turning ashen grey, and he said, "I don't feel well."

"Let's go to the doctor's, then!" said my mother.

"No, I don't want to go there."

"Let me go fetch him."

"No. Maybe I'll go there tomorrow, if God wills."

"You speak strangely, let me go."

"No, it's no big deal—everything will happen the way God wills it."

My mother didn't look pleased at his conversation and she left for the bedroom. In the doorway as he was leaving the living room, he looked long, sadly, at Ivo, who continued reading the comic books, and at me, as I patted the purring heathen goddess. He closed the door quietly.

In *The Secrets of Paris* I read about drunks and wondered what it was like to be so drunk in a cellar that you sing without noticing that you are doing it. I fell asleep, the book sliding out of my hands.

Late at night, I heard a scream. Ivo was shaking me violently. "Father's dying!" he shrieked.

It was pitch black in the room. I sprang out of bed, and both of us ran into the bedroom of our parents. "Where's Mother?"

"Gone to get the doctor."

There was a feeble light from the night table casting an orange hue over our father; the corners of the room stayed dark. In the double marital bed, two beds put together, he lay in his striped blue and grey pyjamas. His grey chest hair stuck out through the unbuttoned top of his pyjama shirt. He was propped up on a pillow. His eyes were closed and he breathed slowly, inarticulate sounds coming from his throat. Above the bed was a photograph, their wedding, framed in wood: he—in military uniform—and my mother at their wedding, cheek against cheek, both of them handsome and unsmiling.

His breath was partly a snore, partly a sort of choking. His face was pale, and as he hadn't shaved that day, his chin was blue and grey. Ivo and I were so terrified that we couldn't go to his side of the bed; we went to out mother's side. We started screaming prayers, whatever came to our minds, to the Heavenly Father, to let our earthly father live. We had been taught to keep our eyes closed when praying. So I was closing my eyes to pray, and opening them to see how our father was. His gurgling noises came from his throat, as if he were using a mouthwash. White foam appeared on his lips, and began to trickle down his chin from one corner of his mouth. We shrieked.

"God, don't kill him!" I yelled.

"God, let it be your will to let him live! We cannot change your will, but make it your will, if ..." Ivo shouted.

A drop of blood trickled from our father's nose, onto his moustache, and from it onto his chin, and it dropped onto the hair of his chest. A loud breath came out if him, and it lasted long, without him drawing in another, and when the body was silent, again, some more air wheezed out of his throat and red foam appeared in the corners of his lips. His head dropped forward. Ivo and I grabbed his left hand. He had taught us where to find the pulse, hoping we would wish to become doctors in order to find all about the ways of the heart. I pushed Ivo's fingers away, so I could feel, he pushed mine, so he could feel. No pulse. His hand was cool and swollen. Ivo, green in face, pressed his palm against Father's chest, kneeling on the empty side of the bed.

"Nothing! His heart's stopped!" he shouted. "It's finished."

I looked at the clock next to the preserved cherries and blackberries on the dark brown cupboard—grains slanting into trapezoid forms. The large hand of the clock covered the small hand.

"Midnight!" I shouted. "And it's the midnight between the sixth and seventh days of the month! Isn't six the number of the man, and seven the number of God?"

"Yes! Yes! That means he went to God!" Ivo said. "That's a sign!" We stared at his face. It bore no expression, neither joy nor sadness, neither peace nor war; he looked as if he were listening to something attentively with his eyes closed, like an icon in which ears and not eyes see you.

Ivo said, "Look!" and pointed at a piece of paper—Father's handwriting was on it, in blue ink. "In his last hour, when Mother had gone to the doctor's, he called me and asked for a piece of paper. He wrote down his will calmly. See, his handwriting is no different from usual—just read, see how clear his mind was!

"Then he said, 'Look, I will die very soon. Don't forget to love God with all your heart, mind, and soul, don't ever forget that, and all else will come from it. Let us pray.' We began to pray, he prayed for all of us, except for himself. Then he grew quiet and closed his eyes and began to breathe heavily. I began to pray for him aloud. He opened his eyes, and said, "Not for me, pray for yourself! You are remaining on earth, and now leave me in peace, I must breathe out my soul to God.' Then he lay back on the pillow, like now."

My body trembled and my teeth chattered. I looked around as if to find a getaway, but the windows and the door could not do. There was no way out.

"So I prayed again to God to spare him," said Ivo. "He opened his eyes once more, and said, 'I am going!' He meant he was going to heaven. He said it with certainty." Ivo's face was yellow-green and his eyes slanted, as if he had changed his race to Mongolian. "What will become of us?" he asked me. Our father lay no longer a man but a corpse on the bed; blackness of the night was seeping in through the windows. The clock ticked like a time bomb.

We went into the living room, turned on the lights, and didn't dare to leave the room. I prayed to God to revive my father as He did Lazarus—I would serve Him all my life then. Yet I was scared that Father would indeed be brought back to life, but not be the same as he used to be; instead, he might have something heavenly in him, something that would kill me on the spot as soon as I beheld it, turning me into ashes.

The doors opened. Mother, wet from snow, came in with the doctor. Ivo and I stood in the middle of the room in our long spacious flannel pyjamas, with broad blue vertical stripes, in the fashion of Turkish soldiers from an old picture book. With the doctor came in the stink of tobacco and booze. "Where is he?" he asked without breaking his stride.

"He's dead," I said.

"But where is he?"

"He is in heaven!" said Ivo. "You won't find him anymore."

"Oh, my God," cried our mother in an unearthly chilling way. And she ran with the doctor following her into the bedroom. We watched from the door. The doctor listened with his stethoscope, searching for sounds on the chest of our father. "It's too late!" he said.

Our pale mother said, "My God, what will I do with these ones?" and looked at us. Besides being terrified, I was scared, if that makes sense, that aside from a big fear of death, I had a smaller fear, of the future. How would we live? The doctor walked out, his chin on his chest, and several men walked in.

The man who used to help my father make clogs, Marko, opened his mouth as if he would say something, but he said nothing. The uncle, a hefty man, breathed heavily, went to see the corpse and stayed there for a long time. He came back and grunted, as though he were asleep and snoring. He lifted me onto his knee and rocked me up and down thoughtfully. His whole chest rising and falling, he said, "One thing is the other life, and another this life, and we don't have him anymore."

When Ivo and I went to our bedroom, Ivo switched off the lights, and I switched them back on. "Why do you want the lights on? You can't sleep with the lights on."

"I'd be scared in the dark," I said.

"What more is there to be scared of?" he snarled.

"I want the lights on," I said, and he let me have my way. Soon he was wheezing, asleep. I couldn't sleep. What if I die too? I couldn't breathe well. Maybe I am dying? No, children don't die just like that, unless they have a high fever. I touched my forehead, and it felt cool, but feelings could lie. But why should fever be dangerous? Fever should be healthy, the farthest away from death—death is cold. I shivered under my covers. I looked at the window—a big blue-black square in the wall. I propped myself up in bed, realizing I wouldn't be able to sleep, realizing my father had died in this position. I lay on my side, but the black windows behind my back disturbed me; when I faced them, they disturbed me even more.

What if God doesn't exist, and here we are almost envying our father for having died a holy death? I looked at Ivo with envy. See, he's a good Christian, he has peace. He has seen the whole death, and I missed it. When I came in, Father was no longer conscious; maybe he was already dead, or in the last stretch of dying; perhaps he would have told me something, the way Jacob told his son Joseph.

Still, the way it was it seemed it had to be. I felt ill in my stomach, and didn't dare to move out of my bed, lest I should injure the holy balance of reality, its finality.

I heard firm boot steps on the staircase, and then in the corridor. My older brother Vlado, who had been serving as a physician in the army in Novi Sad, stepped into the room, and said, "I heard it. Don't be afraid, everything will be alright. Why don't you switch off the lights, it's daybreak."

"Look how dark it is." I pointed at the black square in the wall.

"No it isn't, look!" He switched off the lights, and the square changed into light grey-blue. "And if I turn the lights back on, it'll look dark outside, but it isn't." He was in a green uniform, a cap with a red star on his head. He had a benevolent, encouraging expression on his face. Then our mother came in and said, "You know, that lout of a doctor, Slivi, was not at the hospital when he was supposed to be. He had left a message that he was at the Happy Cellar but went instead to the Last Paradise on Earth. By the time I found him, drinking and gambling, Father was already dead." She pointed in the direction of the bedroom with the corpse, tears in her nose. "Cerebral hemorrhage, he said."

Vlado went to see the corpse. He came back and said that it was a heart attack, and that Father could have been saved with a timely injection of adrenaline.

"But he didn't want me to get the doctor," she said. "Everything that happens is His will, he said, and not a single hair falls out without His will. Maybe it's better this way. He had ruined his health—two years in the army before the war, five in the war in the rain, sleet, snow, and sun ruined his kidneys. He had taken so many medications for kidneys, high blood pressure—his heart loomed so large on X-rays that it always astonished doctors. And then the religious seizure—he did not even sleep, he prayed and prayed for the last two months!"

"He could have lived on—a large heart is not necessarily a terrible thing," said Vlado.

Now it was bright outdoors and we switched off the lights. The sun began to shine.

I walked out of the house and sat on a felled tree trunk—and with my thumbnails I peeled the rugged bark. The windows on the house loomed black. My mother called me in for breakfast. Nauseated, I put my finger on my tongue.

A friend of Ivo's, Zoran, walked into the yard and sat next to me on the bark and peeled the bark. "Now we are the same!" He seemed to be glad—now we could be real friends. His father had been killed while defending a woman from a rapist, who had shoved a bayonet through his chest. Zoran had grown up without a father, without any recollection of him whatsoever. Often in the middle of shooting arrows at trees, playing Robin Hood—he was Will Scarlett; I, Little John; Ivo, Robin Hood—he'd asked me, "How is it to have a father?"

"I don't know how to tell you—I don't know how it is not to have a father."

Now I said, "Yes, now we are the same."

"You'll find out how it is to live without a father," he said.

"Yes."

"But I still won't be able to find out how it is to have a father, and you know that," he said.

"Yes, now I'll know nearly everything I wanted to know," I said.

47

"So we are not exactly the same." He tore a thorn from a roseless rosebush, and cleaned his teeth, pushing the thorn between them, and he did it so violently that he spat blood.

"So we are not exactly the same," I said.

Several hours later more than a dozen relatives in the living room discussed the dead man. My sister-in-law said, "When we saw him last at the train station, he waved to us for a long time, as if he knew he wouldn't see us again. He had joked wittily, played with his granddaughter"—a blond little brat who at the moment dug her fingers into the soil of a flowerpot, and began to knead it into a cake—"and lifted her onto his shoulders. I thought, What a healthy man!" Everybody evoked their last images of him aloud and it was all said in a tone of regret, amazement, and, at the same time, admiration for the integrity of his death. I thought I could contribute. "Ivo shook me out of sleep in the back room, he screamed, 'Father's dying!' I leaped out of bed, and there he was, purple foam trickling down his chin, gurgling noises coming through his throat, and then he choked, and the blood trickled from his nose...."

Everyone in the room frowned. I became quiet. There was silence. I thought I had said something wrong; I put my right shoulder over my chin, to hide my mouth. Yes, they didn't like hearing anything from me; I wanted to impress them with how much I'd suffered and with how much my father had! I should have told them something uplifting, like Ivo when he tells them the religious stuff, like "I am going," and that stuff about the midnight between the sixth and the seventh days.

During the day, my mother washed the corpse and changed it from pyjamas into a suit, his Sunday best, which he had worn on the way to church to preach about the death of Christ. Now, however, he had no hat on his head. His swollen chubby hands with two purple nails (from hammer misses in work) were intertwined as if in prayer, though when he was dying they had lain at his sides. Maybe the hat should be put over the hands, I thought. He lay in a casket on the dining table where he used to sing, joke, and play the guitar as well as tell us Biblical stories, adding to them things that I couldn't find in the Bible, like more and more adventures of Jonah. The undertaker, who had brought the casket with Father's name and age in golden letters, put some disinfecting white dust into Father's ears and nose, and then plugged the ears and nostrils with cotton—to keep the death inside.

The curtains were rolled down. Mother went to the neighbours across the road, to an old woman whose husband, also a clog-maker, had died three years before, and returned with the black flag. I went into the street to see how the house would look with the flag. Above the swallows' nests that Mother had shattered with the flagpole in the fall to prevent the swallows' return in the spring, the black flag came out between the red tiles where Father used to stick out the flag of our Socialist Federal Republic of Yugoslavia. The house looked like the tower of a missing castle, with a very simple and ominous emblem.

I recalled a dream from five years before. In the dream, Father and I sit in the living room next to Mother's casket. He says, We'll have to live without her. Can we live without her? I ask. I think so, he says. At that, I had screamed in my dream, and when I opened my eyes I was relieved that it was dawn. My mother had asked me what was wrong, and I couldn't tell her that I had dreamed she was dead, so I said that a pack of wolves was tearing me to pieces.

Hearing from my father about the prophetic powers of

dreams, for years I had feared that my mother would die. And now Mother and I were sitting with Father's corpse, wondering how life without him would be.

Many people came to pay homage. Mother led them into the living room without turning on the lights. There were no candles at the side of his head. Some light came through the half-opened door and through the curtains. A strong disinfecting smell stung my eyes and nose. And what was the smell there for? To disinfect the dead one from death or from the last traces of life?

I wanted to touch my father again, but I couldn't, as if death in him would devour me too if I touched it. His cheeks were growing purple; the capillaries around his eyes were breaking open. His chin was covered with white and black stubble. Yet he still looked somehow good-natured and attentive, with his arched eyebrows and the clean parallel lines on his large forehead. His relatives and friends gathered around the casket. Some crossed themselves. Some wept. It made me glad to think that others were sad too, but I wished they wouldn't stare like that—it was obscene, they looked at my father as if he were a new species. Ivo and I stood in the corridors all day long and asked each other, "Do you want to see him one more time?"

"I think I couldn't anymore," we would say and go back in.

The day of the burial arrived, cold and windy. "This is your last chance to see him," our mother said to us. She walked to the casket and kissed Father's purple corpse, her tears dropping onto his ear. The mortician, a dry bony man whose moustache was white on the sides and yellow beneath his nose from smoking, said, "Time to go!" He seized the casket cover, which had been leaned against the wall like some great gilt shield, and laid it atop the casket. He took a hammer and nails in his hands. Vlado snatched those away from him. As a child Vlado had worked with hammer and nails, helping with the work of nailing leather onto the wooden soles. Even Ivo and I had had to do it, and several times we had stayed up all night to meet the glass-factory deadline; we all took pride in being the best hands with hammers and nails.

Vlado hammered the nails through the yellow metal holes on the side of the cover. He hit with measure. Both the living man who was hammering and the dead who was being hammered in must have hammered millions of nails each, the dead one more than the living one. The sound of the hammering was dull; there was no echo from box because the box was full. Our mother wanted to take Ivo and me out of the room so we wouldn't witness this, but we wouldn't let her. I wondered why I wasn't crying. I could barely breathe, there was pressure on my chest, and my body was cold and electrified.

Four people carried the casket through the doors, down the steps of white, black-spotted stone. Masons from the Dalmatian Coast had made the steps, smoothing them out for days, and they had shown me pictures of women's pubic hair, and I hadn't believed them. I had thought women had pearls in shells there, not hair. The crowds parted before the casket like the waters of the Red Sea before Moses. The casket was carried through the varnished oak door of the house entrance into the yard, with the carriers maneuvering and panting as if with a heavy piece of furniture. There was a crowd waiting next to the thorn bushes, next to the cherry trees—no leaves—and next to the flat wall of our neighbour's house.

That wall carried no windows except a small one of the larder, with iron grates over it. People used to point their fingers at our neighbour—he had been in the wrong army during the war. Now he stood against the wall, grey, ghastly, as if waiting to be shot by a firing squad. In the midst of the yard stood a black hearse with a silvery cover. Two black horses with blinders stood in front of it, and steam rose from their backs, from the areas not covered by black satin. They did not move their tails—probably the function of tails is mostly to chase away flies, and in January there were none. They bowed their heads, as if there were grass among the wet gravel, or as if they reacted to the human emotion and gave it even better expression than the people could. The casket screeched onto the hearse. The horses moved their ears as if the noise had tickled them. The screeching brought a chalk whiteness to my sister, Nella, who had just arrived from West Germany, where she was studying to become a nurse. I used to irritate her by driving big pots over cement, because I knew that she hated the screeching of dry chalk on blackboards, and pots on the cement. Men in black, a variety of relatives, hooked green wreaths with purple tapes onto the feeble top frame of the hearse.

A procession formed. Mother, two brothers, I, and two sisters stepped behind the hearse, and behind us, three uncles and five aunts. One uncle was missing because he had loved cars so much that, as the first mechanic in town, in the middle of the winter he had lain on the ground beneath the cars and had caught pneumonia and died. I chose to walk next to Nella rather than Ivo. The procession was very slow. Now and then I turned around to see how my uncles were. They all looked thoughtful. The steadfastness of the pace held a lesson for us, some lesson anyway, as we shifted from one leg to another. Howsoever slowly we went, by howsoever many places, we could not deviate from the crooked path that led into the graveyard. We went across the railroad tracks, the casket bumping up and down. Then over a hill, past the shabby house where Father and his nine siblings had grown up. As the oldest son, he had helped his father in clog making and had attended only four grades of elementary education, though he'd been declared the best pupil of his class two years in a row, and though the school principal himself besought my grandfather to give his son a chance. "I'd be delighted to," replied my grandfather, "If you, Mr. Principal, replaced my son in the shop to feed all these children." The grandfather had died of cancer—because of his strong faith in God he had refused to go to the hospital to have a growth removed. The house had been sold a long time ago. Now in the backyard many white geese greeted the funeral with hissing. We walked around the cemetery onto a hill with three crosses in imitation of Golgotha: Jesus crucified between two robbers. Jesus was missing, somebody must have stolen him. But the robbers were on the crosses, white pigeon paint making strips down their cheeks, as if they were weeping.

The Baptist cemetery was fenced off from the Catholic and Communist cemeteries—the Eastern Orthodox cemetery was on another hill—corresponding to our isolation in the community. Wherever we went, fingers pointed at us and hushed whispers followed us; we were called the "new-believers" in derogatory tones of voice—meaning the "wrong-believers."

The hearse got stuck in the muddy ditch between the road and the Baptist cemetery. The coachman whipped the horses with a thin leather whip to inspire them to pull the hearse, and the hearse nearly toppled over. My three uncles and a grave digger carried the casket off the hearse. The horses pulled the hearse out of the ditch. They bowed, staring at the ground, but now and then they lifted their heads and watched the burial with their large moist eyes, their foreheads contorting into sad, thoughtful expressions.

In the Baptist cemetery wooden crosses, cracked from heat, rain, and cold, tilted in the soft soil, the names erased. Others, made of old thin stone, collected moss on their northern sides, as though to protect them from the winter winds. Ivy climbed them snakily, making them resemble the emblem of medicine. Some graves did bear tombstones, but most of these had sunk half their height into the soft earth and dry weeds grew around them. Over the edge of the hill on the western slope, facing the "Whore of Babylon" (as the minister called it), Rome, the Catholic cemetery sprawled, filled with large stones, marbles, and fat little angels like Cupids—all they needed were bows and arrows. Between the graveyards from several cedar trees pigeons descended onto the ground, probably in the hope of getting crumbs of bread. I took the pigeons to be doves, and their descent a sign from God.

Beneath one cedar two fresh heaps of yellow and green soil arose like wings, and between the wings blinked no bird, but a rectangular hole, the grave. I was glad my father would be buried under an evergreen tree on the highest point of the cemetery—even better than Robin Hood beneath an oak. People gathered all over the soft cemetery, trampling old graves, sinking into them in their best shoes, totally disregarding the ones who had been dead, and paying attention only to the newcomer, or, rather, the new-leaver.

The minister stood right next to the tree, turning his back to the Catholic slope. On his left were about ten members of the church choir. They sang about death, heaven, faith, grace, and all the rest, addressing my father in his coffin. After the singing, the minister shouted a sermon, and some foam appeared over his lips, and trickled down his closely shaven round cheek, which was pink in the wind. The parallel lines of his shiny hair showed the distance between the picks of his comb. "We cannot even sing about how we miss him, because without him we don't have a good bass! We all miss him, but dear honourable citizens and comrades, brothers and sisters, I tell you, there is no point in our being sad, for this man is alive!" Saliva sprinkled out of his mouth like sparks of fire. He paused for effect. His thunderous voice echoed behind our backs from a steep hill, covered with apple orchards, beyond the cemetery.

I looked at the coffin, expecting the lid to break open.

After a hush, there was a commotion and murmur in the crowd, especially at the edges of the crowd, where the non-members of the church, including the Communists, stood.

My toes freezing, I wished the minister would stop his speech—he said we hadn't had such a good death in years, and went into the details of my father's death, nearly verbatim from Ivo's account—there was no way of stopping him. From the corners of my eyes I observed the crowd. My school classmates with our main teacher were there. A couple of girls wept, some boys looked gleeful, others nudged each other with their elbows. They were scrutinizing me and taking bets—whether I would cry or not. I learned that later from a friend. I wished I could throw stones at them. I turned round and stared at the crowds of familiar faces with animosity.

Two grave diggers, who had been waiting impatiently for the speech to be over, shifting their weight from one foot to another in soiled rubber boots, leaning their hands on the shovels, dropped the shovels, and with the help of two uncles of mine, withdrew the planks of wood from beneath the casket and began to lower the casket on ropes into the soil. The casket dropped out of my sight, and I had a sinking sensation, as if my heart had sunk into my intestines. The ropes grated against the casket, sounding like dull saws cutting into wood.

Mother and Grandmother, arm in arm, walked to the grave, and Mother leaned to the ground, picked up a chunk of soil, and handed it to the mother of my father. The old woman tossed it into the grave. A loud thump on the wood. Then Mother tossed some of the soil into the grave too. A loud thump. Great pressure in my chest. Behind my nostrils, below my eyes, it burned— it felt similar to the anesthesia for my tonsillectomy several years before. Having seen the red mesmerizing light and felt the scorching sensation on awakening I had screamed, "Am I in hell?" A doctor had had to intervene because my scream had made my throat bleed.

Vlado and Ivo threw pieces of soil, and so did my older sister Nada, tears flowing down her cheeks. Nella and I refused to throw. I walked to the grave, and Ivo wanted to stop me, pulling at my coat, so that I slid, on the edge, fighting for my balance and staring into the muddy water: atop the casket sat a bloated green frog, a beating heart.

Grave diggers avalanched soil over the casket. The thumps grew less and less loud, and more and more dull. The grave diggers sped up their work, and one of them spat into his fists—as though sealing some good agreement—to avoid getting any blisters.

From the hill you could see how people dispersed, church-bound, or pub-bound, or home-bound. We too walked away from the grave, even though the grave had not yet been filled with soil to the top.

A warm wind lifted Nella's hair from her eyes. When I didn't watch myself, I began to skip my steps, hop. I wondered at the inappropriateness of my cheer. Nella sang "Silent Night" in German.

"Did they pray for you so you could speak in German tongues?"

"No, I learned it from tapes in a classroom."

"That's too bad. Did you see any murders in Stuttgart?"

"What a strange question!"

"I heard Germans were murderers, so I was afraid you'd never come back."

"No they're nice. "

"Impossible. Have you seen our history book? Our people hanging from the trees, houses burned, children shot to death?"

"Those were the Nazis. Modern Germans are very cultured."

"But they kill the soul in Germany and America, my teacher says. They don't believe in God, do they?"

"Most of them do, more than here."

"Uncle Pero says their bread is made of plastic foam."

She continued to sing.

In the church the minister told the congregation they should all hope to die like my father. "Who among us has prayed as much as this man had? I had a quiet minute at his side, and as I prayed for him, a voice whispered to me to stop praying and to look at his knees. I rolled up his pyjamas above his knees—they were coated with a thick layer of blood crusts. So let us give praise to God for such a wonderful death. Our man is now in New Jerusalem."

As soon as the sermon turned to more general terms about the glories of heaven, I began to stick my thumbnails into the bench along the grains. The minister broke the bread, and the electrician passed it around in a small basket; wine followed in a silvery bowl resembling the Cup of Marshall Tito trophy that my favorite soccer club had won. I was glad that I couldn't participate in the ceremony—I hadn't been baptized—because I couldn't imagine salivating on the rim of the cup with a hundred old men and women. I liked the smell of wine, though.

On their way out of the church, a variety of old people stroked my hair with their dry hands—as if dipping their fingers in the sacristy, reverting to their Catholic habits—and the sacristy was my hair.

At home dozens of relatives ate the chicken paprikash and cakes Mother had somehow managed to prepare amidst all the confusion. I knew it was she who did it, because nobody else made such poppy seed cakes, cheese pies, and apple strudels. I laughed though there was no joke being told, my sister told me to stop it, and she pulled out a smooth yellow German toothbrush, and brushed the poppy seeds from between my teeth. That tickled me and made me laugh even more.

The cat, who had been outdoors for three days, scratched her back against my shin, blinked flirtingly, and purred as if everything were in the best possible order and none of us were missing. She could not count; if she had four kittens and two were taken away to be drowned, she continued purring, apparently not noticing that some of her children were missing. But if you took all of them away, for days she would moan so sorrowfully and dreadfully that you had to shudder. There were enough of us left for her. Perhaps soon I too would be used to there being one less among us, to having no father. I slipped her some white meat beneath the table when nobody was watching, and she devoured it without chewing, momentarily interrupting her purring, and continued to blink for more.

Even though Vlado, Nada, and Nella were there, Mother kept repeating that the house was empty, and I agreed—there was more echo on the staircase. "Wherever I open the door, I see him there, sitting and reading the Bible, or kneeling, or pacing around the room," she said.

Mother raised the tombstone to my father. She inscribed my father's name on it—the same as mine, to my displeasure. And to my horror, she engraved her name with the date of her birth, leaving the date of her death empty, so when she died, only one date would have to be cut in the stone. After erecting the tombstone, she walked to his grave almost every other day.

I avoided the cemetery. But willy-nilly I came to the grave a year later after drunk Uncle Pero had fallen off a barn, breaking his neck. The smooth stone, black and spotted with grey, reflected my shadow. And, as became a beekeeper, his tombstone bore a honey-coloured inscription; *Death, where is thy sting?*

I feared the room where Father had died. My brother Ivo didn't. The unsmiling brown wedding picture of my parents stayed above the bed, both of them looking alert.

For years I couldn't eat apples, my father's last supper. When I did try to eat them, I choked. Every 6th of January for several years I remembered what had happened. I kept the lights on then, fearing that I myself would die.

On the first anniversary I was certain that I would die at midnight, though I knew that my belief was irrational. I put Father's Zenith watch next to my bed. I prayed, opening and closing my eyes. Thirty seconds left, ten seconds left. My heart skipped beats and pounded against my chest like a hawk in a glass cage. I was sure the glass would burst in a couple of seconds. When it was a second past midnight, jubilant, I thanked God. And so every year until my reason began to prevail.

I couldn't control dreams. Father would still be in the workshop, made of Styrofoam, lying between two chairs like a magician, without his body bending.

In one dream he appeared in his room and called me to his side. Come, Yozzo, I'll tell you something.

What will you tell me?

You are the only one who knows that I am alive.

But we buried you, you are dead.

Yes, you buried me, but I am not dead. I am about to die now.

For the second time?

For the second time. But first bring me an apple, and choose a beautiful one.

I brought him one that looked like a heart, and pressed my thumbnail into it—it was crunchy.

I walked out and wondered how we could bury him for the second time. What would the police say when we took out his second corpse? How could we hide him? Could we bury him in the garden? When I came back he was propped up on his pillow, the room stank of dead fish, and he, barely lifting his eyelids, said, Son, no rush, I'll be here for months. I am not going to die quickly like the first time.

Nobody knew that he was alive except me, and I kept him in the back room like some monster. One day I wanted to take him out for a walk, but when I touched him, his flesh fell to pieces, scattered on the white sheets, without any blood.

RUTH'S DEATH

It's hard for me to write about parents since I know more about children than about parents. That is because when I was a child, I was more interested in myself and my siblings than in my parents, and now that I am a parent, I find our children more interesting than us parents. I remember my parents saying I would understand what they said when I grew older. I still don't understand them. My father died when I was eleven and I was a bit estranged from my mother because Father and Mother made a simple game—I was his favorite, and my older brother Ivo was hers. (She was still alive, eighty-seven, when I wrote these lines, and now that she has died I'm rewriting.) She had been ill now for five years. We expected her to die after her heart attack, stroke, diagnosis with diabetes, food poisoning, and herpes shingles which gave her chronic neuralgia. Jeanette, our two children, and I, went to Daruvar for her birthday party, May 27. Her middle name was May; she was born in the States, in Cuyahoga County, in 1918, way before the river went up in flames.

She was paler than usual, her hair, which had stayed half black until her eightieth birthday, was now completely white, her green-hazel eyes seemed to have grown smaller although they had always been small, under high-arched eyebrows, and she looked startled, caught in a role she didn't like. She had seemed to be the strong one, taking care of the others who were sick, and this change surprised her.

As we slurped tomato soup, my daughter, who was three years at the time, asked, Are you a ghost?

Mother, who could understand some English, having been born in the States, and having spent her first three years of life there, wanted us to translate. (She could sing "Mary Had a Little Lamb" before her final illness.)

I said, I'm not sure I should translate.

Why not? she asked. She looked like a turtle, with all the creases and ancient caution, as though I could harm her.

Well, she asks whether you are a ghost. It's quaint how a child sees things.

My mother didn't seem to find it quaint. She didn't laugh, didn't comment. She gave me a look with her shrinking head, and I felt put in my place in this biology of life and death. Who the hell was I to tell her about life and death? Mothers took care of survival.

I felt I needed to explain more, and I said, See, we told her that you were gravely ill and that we should rush to see you before you die.

So, when will she become a spirit? asked my daughter. I am the first person in the world Eva saw, as my wife had a C-section, and I think that she still trusts me in the primary-imprinting kind of way.

What did she ask now? Mom asked.

I translated again. Eva had her own theology, that everybody dies, but first becomes a ghost, and gradually, when the ghost learns how to fly very well, it quits hanging around the body, dies for the second time, and goes into the heavens, and when it has nothing to do with the body, it is a spirit, spirit in the sky.

Your grandma is fully alive, I said to Eva. She's just pale; that doesn't mean she's a ghost.

But I wanted to see a ghost. I've never seen one.

We slurped our tomato soup in silence, and Eva kept glancing up at her grandmother and grandmother at Eva. Mother had wanted us to name Eva Ruth. None of her grandchildren and great grandchildren had got the name Ruth, and she wondered why. I said that names sound better when they end in a vowel, which you can enjoy in your vocal cords for a long while.

I used to be Ruta for many years, she said, until you all got hold of my birth certificate and saw that I was named Ruth, so I started using my original name. You could have called someone Ruta in Croatian.

Sure, but it sounds like the road. Who wants to be trampled on? I asked, and thought, Holy Cow, what a question. Wasn't she trampled on, like a Route?

We visited Ruth several times, always expecting her to die shortly afterward. Once, after her collapse consisting of a heart attack and stroke, we came to Pakrac Hospital, where she lay in a ward. We drove in an old Volkswagen Bug borrowed from a friend. It was winter and the windows couldn't be completely closed and the heat didn't work. We were freezing during the two hour trip through side-roads and damaged villages. Many houses were burned down, but as they were made of stone and brick, they still stood. Some floors and roofs collapsed from the beams' burnout. Many houses had bullet holes in the mortar. We passed through two deserted villages on the way, with thin snow sporadically covering the ground. The hospital itself was mostly destroyed with howitzer and anti-aircraft bullet holes in the grey walls. My older brother Vlado used to work in this hospital as an ophthalmologist and now he worked independently but he still knew the cardiologist who had remained in the hospital. Vlado claimed that the first missile of the Yugoslav war landed in his bed at the hospital. The Yugoslav army surrounded

Pakrac and started shelling the hospital under the pretext that there were Croatian policemen there. A missile went through the window and landed on the bed. As the bed was soft, and the bomb required a strong impact to go off, it didn't explode. My brother was supposed to be there that night and he would have been probably in bed that early in the morning. He had stayed home to pay attention to his sick wife, a woman whose family was obliterated by the Serbian *chetniks* in the second world war, in front of her eyes, and who, despite her initial good looks, remained a sorrowful face, whom everybody shunned.

On the way to the hospital, on the former highway of *Bratsva i jedinstva* (Brotherhood and Unity) we saw bunnies. A large brown hawk sat on a walnut tree. In the hospital yard, crows hopped among chicken. We walked in and asked to see Ruth Novakovi. Kindly nurses led us there. Ruth was sharing a room with two other elderly women. She sat up when she saw us. How are you? I asked.

How could I be? *Svakako.* Any which way. Bad and good.

It's all right here in the hospital?

Yes, we talk and talk. What else can we do?

We know everything about your children, said a woman in the bed next to hers.

And I know everything about her extended family. It's like a conference of biographers here, my mother said. All that remains after so many of us is stories.

Good that you can remember so many lives, I said. I would make a terribly boring patient. I'd have to resort to telling jokes.

That would be sad, Mom said. There's more to life than ridicule.

We wanted our son to play the cello for her.

He doesn't have to play for me, she said.

He will anyway, I replied. It was a small cello and he made a beautiful sight and sound, so little as he was with the little cello, with long blond hair, stringing out various études.

How do you like his playing? I asked.

I am not an expert. I don't understand any of it.

You don't have to understand it—do you enjoy listening to him?

I am too busy thinking about it all, all of you, so many people, to talk about pleasure now.

I remembered now. It was hard to get a compliment out of my mother, and I was fishing for one, obviously. If it never worked for me, maybe it should work for my son. Not that I needed a compliment for me, but I wanted one for my son's well being and my mother's well being, a moment of satisfaction, an insight that life has been good after all because, look at it, the offspring is talented and beautiful. Maybe there was such a moment of satisfaction in her as she listened and breathed heavily. She simply didn't have the means of expressing that satisfaction verbally and the habits dominated the patterns of speech especially now— what is the right thing to say as someone seems to be deathly ill? We all floundered, customs didn't seem to provide the necessary ammunition. Ammunition to kill the awkwardness?

But her thinking also couldn't be changed. How much does the cello cost? she asked. How can you pay for all of that? Isn't that reckless of you?

Yes, it is reckless, I said. And it would also be reckless not to spend anything on the cello and children's music education. Remember how our father tried to turn us into musicians, how he bought a piano, and then an organ, and a violin, and none of us would play, but here, don't you think he would be delighted if he saw his grandson, if he could see him.

Yes, he would be, she said. He was wild about music. But he was not a realist.

But don't you love music?

Oh, don't worry about what I think.

Well, we don't need to quarrel as there's nothing to quarrel about, I said. Some things are good, and you see we are proud of him.

Poor kid. Do you feed him enough?!

Yes, we do our best.

He should have a little more colour in his cheeks.

He'll get it in the summer.

But where will you be in the summer? I hope not in Russia again.

In Russia, after all, I said. They have more sunshine then than anybody in the summer—white nights.

Oh yes, then you won't be able to sleep.

You've never been much of a sleeper yourself, I said.

No, I had to worry about everything all the time, and now it doesn't matter. If I had known it would all end up like this, I would have slept more. But even that doesn't matter now. It really is all the same.

That's a relaxing thought, isn't it?

I wish I could just fall asleep and never wake up. Being dead would be better than this.

How can you say that?

You have no idea how much pain I have.

From the heart attack?

No, that hasn't bothered me that much. But these nerves on my left side and my back, they feel like I am on fire. That never goes away, no pain killers, nothing helps, and it just grinds me down.

That does sound terrible.

I don't know how that happened. And my brother has the same neurological illness except it attacked his eyes, and he is blind, and he says he feels like scratching his eyes out of his sockets, his eyes itch and hurt so much.

I know, I visited him. At least he follows all the news and discusses politics, more than when he was healthy.

Yes, when he was healthy, he was drunk. I think he was drunk for thirty years, so you couldn't hear any smart idea from him then, and he slurred so badly I couldn't understand what he was saying and when I did, it wasn't worth the effort. I am surprised that he can make so much sense now, that his brain is so good. He sounds like a president.

That's not much of a compliment. Well, for someone who's had a heart attack and a stroke, you seem to be totally alert.

The pain keeps me alert.

Maybe pain is good for you after all.

It can't be.

She had other crises, and we rushed to see her and gathered around her, and no longer talked about ghosts. The last time I visited her—I visited six times in three weeks but could never stay for longer than an hour as she would get exhausted—she expressed her love of animals. She always enjoyed cats but didn't ask for one. Vlado, who lived downstairs from her, and took care of her, had a large dog, but no cats and his wife hated cats.

I heard there's a family of hedgehogs living in the bushes

downstairs, she said. One of them caught a birdie which fell out of a nest, a little swallow, and carried it to their lair. It was all naked and hairless, and when Vlado prodded the hedgehog with a stick, it still wouldn't let go of the birdie but ran with it to the other hedgehogs.

That's kind of nice, I said, although it sounded terrible as well.

Maybe it fed its young ones like that.

It's possible. Have you seen them? Would you like to see them?

I probably would but I don't need to. Life like that is interesting. I've seen a lot of life. You know, we lived in the village, where my misguided dad ran a farm, if you could call it that. What a failure he was! But he loved animals, you know. He had many good moments with cows, dogs, cats, goats, geese, donkeys, doves. He loved doves, and his grandson, Pepik, inherited that disease. He had a collection of carriers. Poor boy!

True, my cousin was devoted to letter-carrier pigeons. And this kind of love of animal life was part of our extended family. Just knowing that there was such life around her seemed to comfort her. There she was similar to my daughter who loves animals so much that we have several anecdotes. One: Eva picked up a snake. The snake bit her. Eva cried. Why are you crying? Jeanette asked. Because my snake left me. She slipped into the bushes and I can't find her anymore.

(I wrote this section while Ruth was still alive, and that's why it's in the present tense, in parts.) Mom sits in a house where I grew up, and stays in the room where my father died. It used to be Mose Pijade 43, named after a communist, Tito's adviser in World War II. Now it's named Jelacica 43, after a Croatian Governor, who helped suppress the Hungarian National Revolt in

1948. It's a big house, which took many years to build, made of stone and brick, very solid, although in my dreams the house shows up falling apart, with the walls swelling, moving, warping.

When I visit her I can't stay very long. She keeps her windows closed, other than one, because she's scared of draughts. There's a musty smell there. Since she can't walk to the bathroom, she keeps her large potty right there, and my brother empties it every evening when he comes to make sure she has taken all her pills. That's the smell of old age then. In the States, she would be in an old people's home, and perhaps that would be better, but here my brother takes care of her, and he considers that superior to the alienation of old age. She doesn't need much company and she's among her own, Vlado says, and talks: I know Czechs in this area, who, as soon as their parents are over seventy, no matter what shape they are in, ship them into nursing homes or put them in far away villages, to die alone, like sick cats. That is shameful. I had a patient here, an old Czech, and her son kept asking how long she had to live yet, and was disappointed, clearly, when I said, she could live ten years. In all that, my brother may have forgotten that we are quarter-part Czech ourselves. He's not eager to see Czechs in a good light, apparently. At the same time, it's pretty heroic of him to be taking care of her for years now. His vacations are limited by whether he can find care for her—and now that he is at the coast, he has a sturdy woman in her mid-forties helping out. She's a housekeeper for the old castle in the middle of the park, which used to be a school, where I finished my elementary education; and now it's partly a museum and to a large extent, a wine-cellar. Well, it always had fine cellars from which the smell of old oak, soaked in wine, and rotting slowly, for decades, spread and wafted up the corridors into our classroom. No wonder so many of my classmates became alcoholics, and at least two of them, out of thirty, have already died from alcoholism. That woman now cleans the museum and castle, living with her two sons, without a husband. I met her, and she talked eagerly and loudly, but was clearly good natured, an old style peasant. She comes in three times a day now and delivers the food. My mother eats minimally, half a potato a day, a slice of bread with honey, a glass of milk, a slice of orange. She doesn't move much but keeps listening and looking. She's a bit deaf, so her TV set is loud. She used to be a big reader. In a way she represents the history of culture here and abroad—the defeat of the written word. When I borrowed books from the library, such as *The Village of Stepanchikovo* by Dostoyevski, she'd rebuke me for reading too much and then even before I'd get to read the book, she'd finish it, and would comment on what a waste of time it was.

A cousin of mine, who didn't like to read much, had respect for Ruth, and she asked her for advice, What novel should I read? I am on vacation.

Tess by Hardy is excellent, Ruth said, and the cousin read the book and loved it.

When did you read the novel? I asked her.

Years ago, when my mother and I lived in Zagreb. Mother had divorced Papa, and she took me along to Zagreb, while my little brothers stayed with the stepmother, who, by the way, was an angel. She never had a child of her own, and she had to put up with Papa's pining after his former wife, Mary. Once a week or so he'd go into a diatribe about how much he missed her, and what a mistake it was that he let her go, and Strina never objected to it, but loved him till death.

So where did you live in Zagreb?

Where? What could we do? Mary worked as a nanny for a German-Jewish family, who owned a textile factory near the centre. They liked the idea of raising their children bilingual, and they paid Mary pretty well because of English. I helped in the house with the dishes, cleaning, and babysitting. They had a fine library and I read in spare time, and *Tess* was my favorite.

How long did you stay there?

Not long, just a couple of years. When I got married, I went back to the village, but Mary stayed. When the king of Yugoslavia signed the pact with Hitler, the family talked about leaving, to America, and they offered to take even me along. Your dad had already been in the army for two years but he wasn't coming home.

The Germans overran Yugoslavia, and the gendarmes came to the house and took the family away to the train station, for Poland. They kicked us out into the streets.

What happened to the family?

You know what happened. You know what the beasts did with the Jews. Tears rolled down her cheeks, but she composed herself and went on.

Mary volunteered to join the partisans. She hated the Germans and their Ustasha helpers who kicked her new family out of the house. She wanted a gun, but there weren't enough guns then, and so she worked as a nurse, till the end of the war, and when Tito came to Zagreb near the end, she was his nurse.

Wow, she had quite a lot of adventures, then, I said. Strange, she never spoke to me about any of it in Cleveland, but read hundreds of war novels. She could never have enough of war in her head. And you never talked about it. How come I never heard about this period of your life?

Why would you? You never asked, and you never listened.

Is that where you learned to speak German? Or was it Yiddish? You always seemed to have a strange vocabulary, with words from all over.

Earlier on I stayed with the Brkic family, and they spoke mostly German at home. Anyway, I think those years in Zagreb were the happiest years in Mom's life, strangely enough.

She enjoyed hanging out with guys, that's true, I said. When I visited her in Cleveland (where she returned several years after the war), and when she was old and frail, she would limp to the fire-station a block away, and hang out with the fire-fighters. She talked to them, and they listened, and laughed, and said to me, Your Grandma is a hoot! But she wasn't a hoot with me, she told me nothing. But then you don't tell me everything either. How come I never knew you lived in Zagreb? You could tell me more about the war, I am sure.

I could, I am sure, but I am too tired now.

Anyway, a year later, after seeing my mother, I bought a ticket to see her after my classes at Penn State ended. She seemed to be able to last, but I heard that she couldn't get out of bed and that bode no good. I was sitting in the lobby of Juilliard, where my son was spending the day taking classes and participating in the chamber and orchestral activities, and since I had seven hours free, I was making phone-calls to see whether any of my friends were free to get together for coffee or a stroll in the park. In the middle of my leaving a message, there was beeping, someone trying to call me, and it was my brother from Minneapolis. Vlado called, he said. Mother died this morning.

It wasn't unexpected but it wasn't expected either. Still a shock.

Any details? How did she die? What about the funeral? (That felt now like chatter. Nothing changes Mom's death.)

Apparently, she was a bit better than a few days ago, and even had a meal, kasha or something, and later when Vlado came back to give her medication, she was dead. He thinks she simply fell asleep.

She didn't want to live anymore, I said.

Yes, for a long time she claimed it, but she must have really grown tired of being in bed and not being able to sit up.

Will you go to the funeral?

I don't know—we'll look for tickets, but last minute, it's hard, and they aren't going to wait for us. They will bury her in three days. In this country, it can be delayed, but there, they don't do that, they don't refrigerate the dead.

No yet, anyway.

Oh, shit, what to do? To pull out my son from the classes, and fly? But I hate funerals, they're either morbid and depressing, or duplicitously uplifting. I had just been to a memorial which was presented as the happiest occasion on earth, with lots of smiles and laughs, and I didn't believe the mood. It was a Prozac memorial. Well, maybe it wasn't, maybe the spirit was so uplifting.

I walked around the block of grey concrete, NY Public Library, Lincoln Center, Tower Records ... nothing Ruth would identify with as home. To begin with, this was the centre of New York. She was Cleveland steel trash, fodder for the industry and economy here. I walked and I was dizzy. My step was unsteady, this all was bad; it would be a cliché to have a crisis of nerves now. When someone dies, how original can you be? Ignore the death? Indulge it by losing it? What the hell can I do? I know, this is all normal. We will all die and it will be all normal. This is the illness for which there is no help. Religion? Should I pray now? I spent half of my youth in religious frenzy, but where is it now? No, I am not going to pray. It would be an opportunist moment. Maybe I will pray in a month. Maybe I will gather enough faith for that. Now I am just plainly ill.

I went out and re-parked the car from the metered slot into a yard, and I sat there, and didn't feel like getting out of it. I called up my wife, to see whether she could dig up some cheap last minute fares to Croatia. She didn't think I should go— maybe it would be better to have a memorial service some time in December and we could all gather then?

The cheapest ticket at first was $2400 for flying out the same day. Yes, one should not think of money in a moment like this, but in addition to all, this would turn out to be a financial blow. In many American and other national "good families" people grieve and then inherit a chunk of property. A friend of mine from California bought a huge house in England; his mother had died, and now he's happy, and he just got married in his new spacious home. In a way, he made out. My brother would inherit the section of home where Mother lived but he had earned it tenfold—nothing could repay him the ten years of constant care in his best years. I wasn't thinking of all that at that moment in New York as I walked around dizzy, but I did want to get a cheap airfare to Croatia, not to end up not only grieving but also bankrupt.

We had recently gone to Jeanette's father's burial, and then we all drove, the whole family, the four of us, to Nebraska. It was winter, a cold day. Her father had frozen to death. He insisted on taking a drive on the coldest day in December, with his wife, to look at the pastures where he used to have a herd of cattle. The cattle grazed for forty years with his help; he left them in the fields mineral supplements, large blocks of salted stuff which the cows loved to lick, and I helped him with that. Somehow, he never had a four-wheel drive, and he managed to navigate through mud and snow in the hills with his Toyota pick-ups. Now he got stuck in a snowdrift, and his wife went to town to get someone to pull them out, and by the time she got back, Ken was dead.

I had received the news; Jeanette's Mother had called, Ken passed away. How and when I asked and she told me the story. I called Jeanette at her work, and said, Your father died. (I never liked the expression passed away, or the recently fashionable, passed … Death can't be softened.) She broke into tears and rushed home. I cancelled my flight to Colorado College and we drove. When we got to Creighton, Jeanette wanted to drive by the morgue, and there in the window, she saw the sign, Kenneth Baldwin. Up till then we had kept up a reasonably cheerful conversation, even occasionally praising the fullness of life Ken had had, doing all he had dreamed of, even visiting Croatia and Greece, and Alaska and Mexico. As a self-made cowboy, he tended Westward more than Eastward, and I was seen by the cowboy family, when we lived in Nebraska, as an alien element, and I never seemed to fit in, which didn't bother me, nor them—they liked it that way, Europeans, stay away. Anyway, Jeanette broke down when she saw the sign late at night after the long trip. We drove through the little part of Creighton, Nebraska, with all sorts of exhibits—elves working, Santa riding through the snow, happy sights for children, but death made it all appear mechanical and hollow.

Oh, but it isn't this death that I'm writing about, deserving although it is as my mother's death of particular attention. I wondered, why should I take my mother's death more stoically than Jeanette her father's? What is it? Was I trained like that? I knew that Mother would want me to take it stoically, that is how she took her husband's death—even though for years she kept visiting his grave and leaving flowers there. I suppose I was trained—tragedy was the norm, and when I was a kid, after my father died, two of his brothers did (one in the saddle, another drank too much during a harvest and fell off a barn and broke his neck), and many other relatives, and I quit going to funerals. There were wars, there were all sorts of repressive governments, there was inevitable misery, that was the family ethos, and to top that, we were Baptists, so death was a challenge we would transcend through faith. Anyhow, she is dead, so how I react makes no difference to her. It won't get her to heaven, it won't bring her back to life. It's only for me, how I would feel now. I feel terrible, and I don't need to feel better at the moment. Well, I don't need to deceive myself. For years I was getting used to the idea of the entropy of her life—she could do less and less, her valves were gone more and more, after several heart attacks, her muscles could do less and less, and finally I could not even call her. She would be there but she had no strength to pick up the phone.

Once the phone fell from her hands and she didn't pick it up again.

On her eighty-eighth birthday, as most of us tried to call her, she didn't answer the phone. After the first attempt to get to the phone, she fell on the floor, and later she fell again, and had to go to the hospital, with a concussion.

And yet somehow she still stayed alive, and the family enjoyed the idea that everything else was failing but her brain was lucid and intact.

But while I was in Russia after her birthday, Vlado reported that her brain in CAT scan showed signs of shrinking.

I was stuck with a strange visa, so I couldn't leave Russia for a month, and then she was better, but not well enough to take a longer visit, and my brother Vlado was not encouraging it. It would stress her out. She needed calm.

But what does she need it for?

To get better.

Does she want to get better?

I work on the assumption that she does; I can't work on another assumption. I can only help her live, not help her die. I am not Dutch. They believe in euthanasia. For my part, I believe there is no good death. No matter how it takes place, it is miserable. I want to help her live as long as possible.

That's admirable, but still, perhaps she'd like to see everybody and then die?

I imagined if she saw everybody, she'd die from exhaustion. But you've been here several times to see her—I don't think you need to come again.

And so I didn't. I did think she couldn't last, so I bought a ticket to see her in December, after my classes. I thought she could hang in, she had hung in for so long.

Later, when Ivo and I talked about her life, we rationalized a little, not necessarily excusing our not visiting more. She was not into celebration. If you came there, she would wonder how much money you spent, and she would regret such unreasonable living. Could you save that money? Don't you think you should buy some property? How will you live in old age if you have nothing? Why keep travelling? What's the point?

Well, I came to see you.

That sounds fine, but we can talk on the phone and you can send me pictures.

True enough, she had pictures of the whole family, on the cupboard, and she loved getting those, and she spent a lot of time looking at them, and if she had a visitor, when she was still hale, she'd show the pictures and explain who was who. And she could keep the extended family tree all intact in her head, better than anybody, without ever writing anything down.

But she seemed to treasure visits indirectly, and to talk about them years later; however, at the moment of the visit, she expressed only skepticism, and then, criticism, why are you so thin (or fat), why don't you exercise more, why don't you take better care of yourself, do you need to drink at all, and why don't you go to church, it's a shame, all your ancestors were such believers, and you are going to quit that tradition? What gives you the right. And so on. I found it hard to take the criticism, although I should have taken it in stride as a way of talking, not ill meant. And maybe there was some wisdom in the remarks. Not that I would change, but yes, that was the point, somehow she always wanted the change, for the better to her mind.

She never wanted to praise. She didn't praise my son, and she never praised me for publishing my books. In fact, she didn't read them. They were in English, after all, and when they were translated, she could no longer see well enough, but she also didn't want to have them read to her as she didn't have much faith in what I'd say. It would have been far better if he hadn't dropped out of med school, she said. It looked like he would become a reasonable and productive person, and then he dropped out and went into this fantasy world, which does nobody any good. Nobody reads any more and nobody needs to, so why are you writing? You can only disgrace the family like that, with some *psine*. In Croatian, that literally meant nasty dog play.

One theory I heard in the family, why she never wanted to praise is this. She had two daughters, after having a son and daughter who lived, and before having the younger set, three of us, my sister Nela, Ivo, and me. These two daughters died, one at the age of one, and the other at the age of four. They were supposedly both beautiful, especially so the four year old, Ljerka. One day, Mother had visitors, and she said to them, Look how beautiful and how smart she is. She can already add numbers.

And people looked at her, and said, You are right, she is beautiful and smart, an extraordinary child. She will have a great future.

But soon after the guests left, Ljerka turned blue from meningitis, and died.

That was a big blow. Out of four children, two died.

My father's brother, Pero, named his daughter Ljerka, to comfort his brother, and to say, life goes on. There's a beautiful and smart daughter. So, when we were born, Mom didn't praise us, and she made it a scrupulous principle, not to boast of her children. She would be proud, but would keep it to herself. Sometimes her eyes would flicker knowingly, but perhaps she was afraid to acknowledge it.

Instead, especially so with me, because she actually had a good reason to be critical, she would scrutinize me skeptically ever since I had TB at the age of six. I suppose to her mind I was a goner then. I was thin, tall for my age, and I spent a year in fevers and coughs. I pulled through it, and became a strong kid, jumping from trees, wrestling with boys my age and a year older and winning. When I was nine and ten, not a single summer day could pass without my getting into some kind of fight. But she didn't like that symptom of physical well-being: I was wild. And then every winter I had bronchitis, sort of a bad habit of my lungs, and coughed mercilessly for months at a time, trying to suppress the cough in the down pillows, and when I slept, I sweated and drooled. If I coughed at night, she would turn the lights on and look at me with displeasure and sorrow. Why don't you cover yourself better? Why did you walk barefoot? Why don't you take more syrup? Why won't you drink chamomile? Somehow she could impart it to me that it was my fault, a moral failing, that I was afflicted with various childhood diseases. I was a good student, but she didn't expect that to last, and it didn't. This skepticism was also the way she treated my father, who, when partisan officers came over to her place when she lived in a miserable basement, and said, Your husband is now a communist fighter, you deserve better quarters, she replied, Oh, is he now? He left his old army? You know, it may not last. Knowing him, I think he'll give up your army too. And she refused to get a three bedroom apartment from them as she couldn't trust the change of fortunes.

She didn't want much, and she didn't expect much. It was maddening for me that she expected so little and that she worked so hard.

When my father died, she took over the business of making wooden clogs, and worked day in and day out, and she also gardened, raising all sorts of produce, and she cleaned the Baptist church, took care of several old and sick women for free, cooked for us, woke up early to put wood in the stoves, and so on.

The strange thing is that she died in the same room in which her husband had died thirty-nine years before. She did not remarry and she stayed faithful to his memory. I don't know why, whether she was tempted to remarry or not, whether she thought it would be a disgrace to do it, but she stayed alone from the age of forty-nine, which is very young. After all, I am fifty when writing this.

In my childhood, I considered the bedroom of our parents a secret chamber I wasn't allowed to visit without knocking, a terrifying chamber. And it became even more terrifying after my witnessing Father's death there. I never wanted to sleep in the room where he died. She had a choice of that room or another, brighter and bigger, but she chose that one, and that is where she slept for all those years, and where she was bedridden for the last two, and where she died. To my mind, that is amazing, to die in the same room. I mean, I'm now in a plane going to Budapest, and then, on to Daruvar by car or train, for the funeral, but anyhow, I'm on the go. I have no idea where I'll die, where I'll live. I may be buried, and probably will be, in the same cemetery, where most of my ancestors are buried, in Daruvar, if there's enough money and time and refrigeration to transport me back there, but I'm not going to speculate on that, and I could end up elsewhere, which would be just fine with me. I'm not that faithful to one location. There's clearly pressure to be location faithful. In my stories, I have written too much about Croatia and Yugoslavia ... Maybe it's enough to have a mental faithfulness to the place. But there are other places now, where I have lived, where I have experienced, where I want to live.

I wrote several of the preceding pages on the plane, to Budapest. I had asked for the exit row for the leg space on Delta, and I got two seats all to myself. The stewardesses politely offered me extra wine and my neighbours politely tried to sleep. The flight reminded me of my travelling to Europe after 9/11, when there was plenty of space on the planes but also an aura of suspicion and depression. And I was thinking, I don't know what it will be like to see my aging siblings. I am the youngest one. You can get to be the youngest one at the age of fifty. In some countries, it's over the average life expectancy. My father died at the age of fifty-three. In Russia, the average death age for men is fifty-seven. Maybe it's up to fifty-nine, now that nearly all the severe alcoholics who were tempted to die from too much drinking already did so. My oldest sister Nada was an old woman at the age of seventy. She had all sorts of twitches and she never recovered fully from the recent wars.

I used to love landing in Budapest, and taking a break at the baths or in a tavern with gypsy music, but now I had to rush, and I went to the busy Alamo desk where I had a reservation. Next to the counter, a Hungarian car rental representative said, You are better off renting with us. We'll give you a ride, we are only a kilometre away from the airport, and our prices are low: 30 euros a day, including insurance.

Fine, I said and went with the man to a car rental place, which was some 10 kilometres away. To rent a Skoda, the host said he'd have to run my credit card. He gave me the papers, and at first I thought that I had paid a $2,000 USD deposit, in forints, but then when I reckoned more carefully, once I was on the road, I realized that I had put down $20,000. That made me nervous. What if the car got stolen? I'd never get that money back. And how would I find the rental place when I came back? Was the address written anywhere? What if it turned out that they just sold cars that way? You think you are renting, and then you end up with a car, paying twice as much as it's worth?

Normally, I would have turned right back, but I didn't want to miss my mother's funeral. How could I? What is more important in a life than burying a mother? The sun in my jetlag was terribly bright, and the traffic jammed around Budapest as badly as around NYC during rush hour. I kept worrying about the unusual car rental. Maybe it was a good distraction from grief. I drove next to the river Tisza, and it looked green, and the sky hazily blue. The river view calmed me, with slow unperturbed barges, of course, barges. What the hell did they transport? Cabbage?

In Duna, a town on the Tisza River, I went to a gas station restaurant. I parked the car in the lot, using the automatic lock, and walked in. I bought a double shot of cappuccino. It was bitter, so I put in some sugar. Why do Central Europeans save on coffee and serve the cheapest, oldest, raunchiest mud? I looked to the other side of the room, and there stood a statuesque brunette with blue eyes and low cut jeans with pubic hair overflowing onto a flat sun burnt stomach; she had a thin nose, full lips, and graceful hands with long fingers, which she kept moving like a pianist. Why am I noticing this? Aren't I grieving? I better not look at her, it's immoral. When she laughed, her lips revealed terrible dark teeth, some of them obviously rotten. Or were they merely smudged by coffee-mud? No, definitely rotten.

In the States, you'd hardly ever see such a stunning woman, and if you did, she wouldn't have rotten teeth. I was puzzled by the paradox. What else do I need? Water, of course, water. I bought a plastic bottle, and making sure not to look at the rotten beauty, whose melodic voice floated after me, I walked out, and the sun blinded me and disoriented me, and it took me a few seconds to make out shapes. My car wasn't where I left it. I looked around. No grey Skoda. What the hell? Somebody already stole it? Did I lock the door? I talked to a gas attendant. He didn't understand English. He understood a little German.

What is the car license plate?

I have no idea, I said.

What is the rental company?

I completely forgot. It was a strange name, written on a paper in the car. I had a car key, but it had no information, no alarm button. I talked to another gas attendant. I was frantic. They didn't share my excitement. One of them smoked, combed his hair, and looked bored. Probably it happened at their gas station often. Or at any rate, it was nothing unusual in Hungary. Cars changed owners.

Are there police around here? I asked.

Luckily my wallet and passport were on me. The rest was nothing. It's only money. It's only $20,000, why fret? My mother is dead. The hell with money. When you lose, you might just lose as much as you can, and start anew. How will I go to Croatia now?

I walked around the gas station. There was a grey Skoda, much closer to the restaurant than mine, in fact right outside of it. It looked similar to the one I had rented. But this one was a little bigger, and the metal wasn't as new and shiny. I came up to it and looked inside. My black jacket which I had bought for the funeral was inside. Did someone steal my jacket and put it in a similar car? Nonsense. I took out the key and it clicked the doors open. I sat inside, and felt a moment of joy and relief. Shit, am I losing it that badly? What got me? Sleeplessness? Now I drove south and I sped. I didn't care if I got a ticket. So what, I have the car, and what if I have to pay a fine. I could pay 100 or

200, what difference did it make? But what, if in my state of zombiehood, I cause a car crash?

Crossing the border into Croatia was no problem. The trees in early November were colourful, a bit like New England, without the maple red. Rusty red and brown from oaks, yellow from beeches, lots of green from ash, but no red. An old woman was selling shriveled boletes. It is said that owners often resemble their dogs, but perhaps, sometimes old peasants resemble their produce, their knotty potatoes—anyhow, the peasant was somehow as creased and bruised as her boletes. I was tempted to stop by in the woods to gather my own, but I had no time for that—and I recalled how my mother loved to cook boletes with onions. It was perhaps her favorite dish. Wouldn't it be better and simpler if I could just cook a meal of wild mushrooms in her remembrance rather than attend a funeral? She was earthy to the point of being saintly.

It is easy to canonize one's parents, especially mothers. Fathers, it's easy to demonize them. But I was not the only one doing that. I remembered a cousin of mine, who gave me a sermon about what a saint my mother was. She had taken care of his blind mother for years, taken her out for walks, visiting her for conversation. That old woman, Marica, was dead by now. Most everybody among Ruth's friends had died. That happens when you're eighty-eight.

I parked the car on the pavement near the stone walls of our old house, which now belonged to Vlado. Instead of the old wooden gate, there was now an iron one, painted dark red. And once I walked in, I compared the current yard to the old one— no apricot, walnut, cherry and apple trees of my youth, but only cement and dark firs and pines. And no beehives in the back of the yard. How can you go home if the bees and the apples are gone? No, it was not home for me, and that comforted me. There was no need to be back, other than death. Nearly the entire family gathered at the house, which, for my brother's wife was stressful. She has gone through chemotherapy and radiation, and now was undergoing another round of chemotherapy, very weak, so, no wonder, for half an hour she hid in her bedroom. She had taken care of my mother as much as anybody else. When I sat with her alone before the funeral party, while Vlado still worked, helping the nearly blind, she wept. I said the worst was over, no more suffering.

I don't see it that way, she said.

It's a relief for Vlado and you not to have to toil for her.

That is not much of a consolation. The house will be frightfully empty, she said.

You could have renters.

No, it's not the same.

I took a whole week off from work, and I wasn't taking care of the funeral details, unlike Vlado, who worked even on the day of the funeral, a couple of severe cases. He said he could barely keep track of all the details that had to be taken care of, such as *smrtovnica*, the black-edged paper announcing her death to townspeople and listing all the grieving relatives, the closest ones, such as siblings, and direct descendents and their spouses, but not cousins and the extended family. There were thirty-eight listed, and he worried that he would misspell some foreign names, which he did. Casket to order, corpse to be taken to the morgue. Now that is a big change from the way it was done in my childhood. Then, the corpse would be laid out in state, usually in the living room and sometimes in the bedroom. A black flag was posted on the house, and friends and relatives came and visited and paid homage at home, and the relatives sometimes slept even in the same room as the corpse. When my father died, he had stayed in the living room, to my horror, and I felt a terrible relief when he was taken out and put in the ground ... Of course, more horror. Now, she wasn't there in the house. Her smell in the room where she lived for the last twenty years stayed there. It was on the second floor, which may have speeded up her demise. If she had stayed on the ground floor, she would have been able to move, to walk, to keep her body functioning a little longer. It is hard to say what got her, but from food poisoning, she also had a heart attack, and so on, an entire list of illnesses.

Over thirty relatives gathered there—some young ones looked good, dressed formally in black, and it seemed a shame we had never gathered like that while Ruth was alive, other than for my father's funeral, but that was way too long ago, when half of these people weren't born yet. It would have cheered her up, no doubt, to see them all gathered. And it was a shame we couldn't take a picture to show her. She enjoyed looking at the pictures of relatives, and while she never bought an expensive dress for herself, she liked seeing her offspring dressed elegantly, and that was one among many reprimands she'd launch at me, that I was a slob. Now even I was dressed, and it struck me it was a shame she'd never seen me in a suit and black shoes.

The main topic of conversation at the funeral party turned out to be health. A neighbour across the street from us was dying just during the funeral, my niece mentioned. By the time our funeral was over, she too would be dead. Death was hovering in the street.

It was a sunny and blue day. Vlado was the only one who didn't have a black suit but a dark blue one. He had no time to go out and buy a black one. I said, Don't worry, blue counts as a colour of grief, that's what blues is called after. 9/11 was a blue day.

OK, I'll take that, he said.

Unlike in the old style burials with horse drawn carriages, after which we walked through the entire town, stopping traffic, this one was localized to the cemetery. We parked the cars outside it, some of us walked to it, and then gathered around the morgue, and formed a procession which went around the cemetery. Not much time to walk and think. Funeral as a peripatetic activity seems to be the most thought provoking time.

We the siblings, five of us, gathered before and went in to the morgue to examine the wreaths with our names inscribed. I hadn't read what my wreath ribbon said; I couldn't find it, but I trusted Vlado it was there and that the appropriate words were on it.

In the coffin, she looked like a classic grandmother, with a shawl around her head, her cheeks sunken, nose prominent, thin, hooked, and her hands large and knotty, almost larger than her head, which had somewhat shrunken with age. Her hands were pale, almost white, off white. Her eyes, also sunken, were much smaller than when she was younger. There was no spasm on her face, which my brother claimed indicated that she didn't die in pain. She had fallen asleep. Her nerves failing before her death might have helped obliterate the pain of dying.

I touched her forehead. The skin and the underlying flesh was cold and spongy, thicker than I'd expected. Vlado said when he'd found her dead she'd already lost two degrees Celsius, which indicated she'd been dead for two hours as one loses one degree per hour. I'm not sure what temperature she was at, but she was very cold.

Yes, peaceful was good, but peaceful and warm are synonymous, when it comes to life, not peaceful and cold.

Relatives came and shook hands, kissed cheeks, expressed condolences. Glassy and shiny eyed we kept our composure, and perhaps it would have been more difficult if the death had been sudden and if there hadn't been the consolation of the end of the suffering; postponing the death would have led nowhere as she definitely couldn't get out of bed again.

The two women who took care of her when she couldn't get out of bed, feeding her, changing her, washing her, and massaging, they both wept, and talked to her. I saw that before, people trying to talk to the dead in the casket—and it was touching. It was good to know that the people who had known Ruth best in her last days loved her. Often it happens that the old become unbearable and outright nasty and their caretakers grow to resent them, but the attachment and love which these women obviously had for her was good, at least for me, to contemplate. Therefore, I was surprised when I found out that Vlado didn't invite them to the dinner memorial party afterward at a restaurant near the park.

After a sermon which didn't do much for me a choir sang and even though the singing was amateurish, it was painful to hear it. I had heard it at other funerals in my youth. *Zbogom.* Literally, With God, which is used as a greeting when someone leaves for a long time. I couldn't control my chin when I listened to the song. It twitched. And I was reminded how my son, when he was born, after a C-section in Fargo, right after his umbilical cord was cut, cried, his chin twitching, while I carried him to the hospital room.

The morticians, four of them, pushed the cart with rubber wheels, along the cemetery and up the hill. We walked on the asphalted path around the cemetery to the high, Calvary section, where the Baptist graves lay. My feet hurt in the new shoes but I didn't mind that. How long are you staying? Vlado broke the silence of falling footsteps, leather soles hitting the rubbery asphalt softly.

Three days, I said. And you will work tomorrow?

Yes, there's nobody else to take care of the blind.

Are any of the old doctors still working?

Bulajic is still working, he said.

I looked at Vlado, startled that such a name should be uttered during the funeral, our funeral. This was the doctor whom Mother couldn't find during Father's death because he'd been at a tavern rather than the hospital (and in my story "Apple," I patterned Dr. Slivic after him). When I was a kid, I thought I should, once I grew to be old enough, buy a gun and shoot that man, and on some level, for at least ten years, until I finished college in the States, I considered it a failure of my religious upbringing that I wouldn't do it, and through the attrition of time, I had if not forgotten, basically forgiven the man and his neglect of ER duty. It seemed my father's heart had been so shot that it was a blessing to die fast rather than to linger and suffer other heart attacks. He'd had what we all deemed a beautiful death, in full faith in God. Vlado seems to have read most of my thoughts, and said, He is a good man.

Really?

Really. He helps the poor, doesn't charge much; during the war, he stayed to help the wounded in the town and the nearby villages, and risked his life for it.

I thought he was a Serb, I said.

Maybe, Vlado said. He could have run over to Belgrade, but didn't. Montenegrin, anyhow; a real *mensch*. He used to be young, you know, but he has always been a good man.

OK, I'll take your word for it.

There are very few good men, Vlado said.

So now I reflected on how we had had no telephone, how nobody in our street had had one, other than the post office, and the hospital was relatively far. (I had used the telephone for the first time when I was seventeen, and I had feared the black rotary instrument, thinking that if I didn't say Hello properly, the connection would break and I would have to pay a fine.) Probably everybody had known where the doctor on duty was, a tavern which was centrally located and more accessible than the hospital, and we were simply out of the loop, perhaps due to our religious isolation, since we considered taverns off limit to us as a gathering of the godless. Anyway, I had talked a few times with that doctor, at the swimming pool, and once when I asked him, You had a reputation as a playboy, he replied, Unearned, believe me. And recently I went to a party, where I was tempted to chat up a lady, when I noticed that there was a young man on the other side of her, trying to do the same. I looked at him and recognized my son. So, I said to myself, Time to give it up, old man. And that's it for me, my man, no more of that.

True, no more of lots of things, perhaps no more of malpractice either. And it struck me that after two medical malpractice deaths in the family, it was remarkable that Vlado had reversed the recent history. Mother should have died by all accounts when she was eighty, but he kept her alive for ten more years through watching after her, screening the medications, cutting some of it to half the strength to make it possible for her liver to continue functioning, and coming up with various strategies against all odds.

The grave was dug shallow, to place her casket above my father's. It was about five feet deep, and perhaps less. The soil dug out was clay, mostly greenish brown, without many stones. After another sermon and singing, I looked at the grave pit. Yes, dust to dust. There were many flowers all around, and bees landed on them and collected pollen. Bees, yes, there should be bees at this funeral. My father had been a bee-keeper, one of my sisters, Nada, was a bee-keeper, my father's *smrtovnica* had the verse, *Death, where is thy sting?* The bees liked this death. They would sting if I tried to touch them.

The minister, who had spent ten years in Australia and had been a baker before (and had spoken in tongues with my father), turned the eulogy into a sermon, as could be expected, inviting people to accept Jesus as their personal savior in order to die well, rather, to live eternally. I remembered how when my father had died, another minister took it as an opportunity for a sale's pitch—a perfect death, such as everybody should desire, thanks to God. But, let him do his thing. My mother, who was a firm believer all her life, would've understood this, would've perhaps even liked this invitation to faith. She had been a shy woman all her life, she wouldn't have liked this much attention anyway, and the speech turning away from her to divine matters would please her. Attention to her would have embarrassed her. She had a terrible stage-fright all her life.

Vlado thanked the people for coming to the funeral, while holding on to the gravestone with the names of his father, mother, sisters. He gripped the gravestone; he needed to hold on, maybe he was unsteady, but merging with the stone, he was steady, the backbone of the funeral. Mother had her name inscribed a month after Father's funeral, with her birth-year, 1918, and then, the year of death uncut. It still had to be cut into the stone, 2006.

Vlado was the first to throw in a fistful of soil, and it thudded on the wood softly. Ivo picked up a fistful from the same heap and a soft thud followed. I suppose I wanted to be a bit less imitative, so I picked up a chunk of soil as large as my fist from the far left and dropped it after looking down into the pit. The sound that came out surprised me. It was sharp, loud—I had thrown a stone coated in soil. This was an aggressive sound of stone-throwing. I recoiled from that. That wasn't what I'd intended. The other siblings threw in the soil and some grandchildren did. Her brother was absent, bedridden in a similar fashion to hers, in Medjuric, a village about forty kilometres south. So I threw a stone at her casket, unknowingly. Does that symbolize what kind of son I was? I wondered.

There was no sensation of relief once it was all done. It's all done, the suffering is over, she is in a better world, I felt none of that. *Death, where is thy sting*—it would be good to know where exactly, but this sting is diffuse, in the veins, arteries, general blue tone of the day, a blue vein without oxygen. Perfect day. We all got a sun tan at the funeral. I had also caught a terrible cold. I wondered whether I'd gotten it the moment I touched my mother's chilly forehead.

I gazed at the stones with family names. There were already two Josip Novaković's buried here. My mother should have, by her matrilineal heritage, been buried at the Calvary cemetery in Cleveland where her mother and grandmother are buried or in Medjuric, where her father is, by train tracks, and where her brother would be buried—he was already dying, in a house, only a stone-throw away from his father's grave.

I walked back with my half-aunt, Djurdjica, who talked about Rutica (Ruthie): Her teacher says she was the smartest pupil he had at the school in thirty years, by far. You never know what she could have become if she had been allowed to continue school after the fourth grade. She could remember everything, she spoke three languages fluently, she could do long multiplications and divisions in her head, and she could think clearly. And then I heard your father was like that in his school and he couldn't go on after the fourth grade. You are so lucky to get such genes. You and your siblings should all be geniuses.

I suppose we should be, I said, but you never know what environment and spite can do to your head. I didn't say that but in my case with lung afflictions and oxygen deficiencies and sleep disorders, I'm sure I got my brain damaged somewhere along the way, not to live up to the genetic code potential.

Djurdjica continued, But the odd thing is that Mother was so shy that when her teacher invited a government official from Zagreb to show how well his pupils were learning, Ruthie wouldn't answer any questions. She turned red and practically mute. The teacher was embarrassed.

Later, after a dinner during which no alcohol was drunk, I talked with my brother and had two glasses of red wine. For a long time my mother had one drink a day and then she lost the taste for it. Djurdjica's mother lived to be ninety-six, and she started every day with a shot of plum brandy. My mother had me taste beer when I was twelve. It had been a terribly hot day, and she sweat in the garden, and said, There is only one thing that will quench thirst in this dog heat, and that is beer. Go out and buy us a large bottle of cold beer.

I did that, and she drank half of it, and wanted me to drink the rest, and I found beer bitter and heavy. I don't like it, I said. It would be good if you never do like it, she said, but you will, you will.

During the evening after the funeral, Ivo brought up his theory why our Mother didn't believe in praising her children, Ljerka's early death.

Do you know the whole story of her death? Vlado said. I was fourteen then, old enough to follow what was going on. Ljerka got the German measles inoculation. The medicine arrived form the United States. Tito had usually declined donations from the States, and it would have been good if he had declined this one. The inoculation was at the experimental stage, and Americans experimented in the countries where there was no system of lawsuits for health damages, and Yugoslavia was one of them. Eighty children in Yugoslavia developed meningitis and died as a result of this overly strong inoculation. (The inoculation would be modified and approved only thirty years later.) Ljerka was one of the victims. Our father went insane over that. When she got sick, he took her to the hospital, and gave a huge sum of money to the doctor, and said, Do all you can to keep her alive for me, will you? The doctor promised he would.

She died the next morning, there was no helping her.

He was struck with grief as was our mother. Only months later did it cross his mind that he had given the doctor a fortune to keep Ljerka alive. The doctor should have had enough conscience to return the money but he didn't.

Father sometimes said, Here I toil for the money I used to have, but those doctor crooks kept it.

So, that's America for you. An American preacher later when he heard the story told our father that he should sue the American government for sending faulty medication to Yugoslavia, but Father declined to do that. He always stayed insanely pro-American.

I wondered if I'd known this story earlier, whether I would've been so eager to go to the States, which I considered my Motherland, since my mother came from there. She had actually come from a borderland family between Slovenia and Croatia.

(A couple of days later, I rummaged through my mother's papers, looking for my transcripts from Medical School of Novi Sad, and I ran into *smrtovnica* for Lyerka. The death notice was signed by Vlado and Nada, siblings, and not by parents. The parents were probably too devastated to write the note to be posted around the town, so the task fell to Vlado. Even then, he was the one staying calm and reliable in tragedy.)

Funerals are perfect occasions for the participants to draw character portraits of the dead. When I talked about Mother's shyness, Ljubica, Vlado's wife, said, Oh, she wasn't always shy. I remember how you threw a truck tire in front of an oncoming car. You rolled it and timed it so it smashed the front of the car. The driver ran after you through the streets and couldn't catch you but you ran out of breath and ran home. She protected you and yelled at him what kind of man he was that he wanted to beat a child. You were bad.

That is true, I remember. I had some delinquent tendencies.

When I mentioned that Mother had a terrific healthy habit of fasting one day a week, every Saturday, Vlado said, She didn't do it for herself. She never did anything for herself. It was for you and Ivo, she prayed and fasted one day a week, so God would protect you and so you'd keep the faith of your fathers.

That is strange.

Yes, you brought her a lot of grief. Well, I must admit, it was not only for the two of you, but for all her children, the five of us, and perhaps for the dead ones too. I do believe it all had a good effect on her health but it was not for her sake she did it. You know, selfishness is basically bad for your health, and altruism is good, and that is why she lived so long, and she would have perhaps lived longer if the last war hadn't shaken her so much.

Ivo and I talked in the living room, while eating layered hazelnut chocolate torts, and I said, You know, we were not good sons. After Dad's death, things were difficult for the old woman and we made them more difficult still by being nasty boys.

I agree, he said. We didn't listen to her at all, we were rude, we stayed in the streets past midnight nearly every night while she worried about what we were doing. We were doing nothing bad, really, we didn't drink or have sex, but she had no way of knowing that.

We thought we were exploring the world, ideas, hanging out with friends, and she didn't understand that.

She didn't approve of our friends, she wanted us to have the square and studious ones, not the delinquents we tended to.

I know, I said. She wanted me to study, but she could hardly ever see me study. I did read books late at night, and she kept coming to my room and turning off the light, saying, you will ruin your sight. What kind of life will it be if you are blind as a mole?

And what kind of life will it be if I am an idiot who has read nothing? I had told her.

But what are you reading? Karl May? What good will it do to you, stupid adventure novels.

It was Einstein's favorite reading in his adolescence.

As was math. I don't see you reading math books.

Get lost! I'll read what I want, and if you want to know, my eyes are my strongest feature—my teeth will fall out, I'll grow deaf, but I will still see very well, I just know.

Don't boast lest God should ...

And we'd quarrel at three in the morning like that. I thought I was in the right, but of course she was. I could've gotten up earlier and read during the day.

And Ivo was like that too, shouting at her. She was a poor widow with sons who shouted at her and didn't listen to her. She carried flowers to the grave of her husband, and perhaps she wished he were alive because we had feared him. He hadn't tolerated insouciance. He beat us to subdue our selfish wills. He beat Ivo more than me and I learned on the example of how to avoid his educational wrath. There was something biblical in his rage—he'd quote from the Bible and beat you. She probably thought we deserved that but couldn't do it, other than, when we were smaller, to pull us by our ears.

Ivo had an anecdote about Mom in exile, in Switzerland, during the bombing of Daruvar. There was an immigrant child, a couple of years older than Ivo's son Matija. The boy, from Serbia, used to beat Matija, the way we grew up, older boys beating younger boys, animal style, older cats chewing on younger cats, something that looks ugly from the outside but is probably an all right way of growing up. You learn to mistrust people and you also learn authority. Actually, I detest that kind of childhood although it was mine. Anyhow, Ruth came up to this boy, and said, Why do you have ears? Why? asked the boy. To listen. I told you not to torture that poor boy, and you keep doing it. That means, you aren't using your ears. While talking to him, she grabbed one of his ears and twisted it. The boy grew red from pain and cried, and she let him go.

Can you imagine if they had reported that to the Swiss authorities, Ivo said. Child abuse. I don't think the boy complained. He stopped beating Matija.

She always took care of her brood, I said. There's something instinctive and animalistic about that, isn't there?

She pulled us by the ear all the time.

Yes, she had a fetish about it. Her favorite saying was an old Jewish proverb. Why do we have two ears and one mouth? In order to talk half as much as we listen.

She believed we should never talk much, eat much, drink much, say much—basically, she asked for a life of restraint and obedience.

True, Vlado said, but she had courage when it came to survival. She saved her father who was in prison for anti-communist statements after the war, when Tito had people shot left and right simply because he didn't want to be weaker than Stalin. He was as ruthless. (Ruth, less? Poor pun, but unavoidable.) She went to the regional communist party headquarters and asked for her father's release, saying he was unjustly accused. Her argument was that he was a worker damaged by America. He had lived in America, worked in a steel factory, joined a union, basically a communist workers' organization, and as an American communist, he was not rational, and his statements therefore should be ignored. He came back to his village, alive, after that. She probably saved him. And then she remained the shy woman and mother. I believe that she was actually quite heroic. Nothing physical scared her. Only people and their politics did, and even worse, diseases.

I remember how I feared, as a child, her death. My second nightmare: my father and I are standing next to Mom's casket. He has blue stubble on his chin. I ask, what next? And he says, How would I know? I wake up shrieking, and it turns out I have high fever. That was my TB year, with lots of fevers.

My first nightmare that I remember, the same year. Ambulance at the gate and mother carried out on stretchers. I shrieked out, *Bonica*. I skipped an *l*, in *Bolnica*, Hospital, or literally, the house of Pain, as Bol is pain. But Bon is good, so, in a way, in my childhood dyslexia, I said the house of good, but it certainly didn't feel like it as I shrieked. My sister Nella woke up first, and comforted me. Now she worked as a nurse in a cardiac surgery unit in Stuttgart. She had been sent to Germany for a training at the age of fifteen, to become a nurse. Why not a doctor, I don't know. She was the best student in her class, but so shy that she often covered her eyes with her palm so she wouldn't have to make eye contact. On the other hand, this is a very ostentatious way of not making eye contact—you can always avoid it, you don't have to use your hands, just look at them. I think looking at your hands at the time of challenge and temptation is the best way to stay put and to tell others to stay put. By the way, my mother's hands were almost as large as her head in the casket. When I looked at her, I wondered why not have *Totenhaende*, death hands imprint, to last forever? I had seen only two death masks, as a pretentious tourist, Beethoven's and Liszt's.

Nella's main complaint about the funeral was that the morticians didn't use Mom's dentures to prop up her mouth. In the West, you won't let the mouth sink like that, she said.

Vlado looked at her blankly. He took care of Mom for ten years, and Nella was never there, and yet often preached about how caretaking should be done. He didn't say a word. So, is that it, your Mom in natural state, is not properly pretty for you? I exchanged glances with him. I trusted him. When Father died, this was the man who came from Novi Sad, as a doctor, with an olive-coloured partisan cap, and dark crimson five-limbed star, after nearly bleeding to death himself from a tonsillectomy gone wrong. This was my father's boy, beaten many times by the man. He was the man now. We were lost without him, and it stayed that way.

I remember how when Dad had died, I looked up at Mother, and didn't say, What's next? It was the end, no father. Even in my nightmare, my father remained as the pillar of safety. But he was no safety. He had no measure in him. She did. I wish she had written as she had wisdom. I don't have it, I never will, my father didn't have it, although he was a luminous and prophetic kind of musician and enthusiast and preacher. He earned her love somehow, so that she remained faithful to him for thirty-nine years after his death, every day looking at their wedding picture. It's amazing. I'm not capable of such endurance, and he probably wasn't, but then, did I know him? Did he know himself? Did he have enough time to know himself? As a biblical pacifist, he spent eight years in the army, two before the war, four during it, two after it, totally ruined by the killing fields. I wonder whether he ever killed. I know he was tormented and tortured. His younger brother boasted that he, as a partisan with a machine gun, had killed lots of people, but was even that true? Dad claimed he shot in the air, that only God could determine who should live and who should die, and he prayed during fire exchange, and he wasn't shot although many people around him eventually were shot.

Now, with the burial over, I realized I wouldn't have to travel to my hometown again, except, perhaps, to die. I always struggled to get away from home, but there was a home, and now there isn't, or it's shrunken into a bit of underground. Eventually, I would have to buy a plot of land near the graves of my parents. That grave looked a little too tight for me. There were way too many people there, in six square metres. Our bones don't need to cling and clang and scrape together; that seemed to me horrifyingly incestuous, way too close. Another plot of land, with some elbow room, although I'm not going to be doing anything with my elbows, would be slightly less appalling than this underground bedroom of my parents.

After the funeral everybody was in a good mood. Ivo, my brother who teaches theology at Baylor, talked so much that he lost his voice. I suppose he couldn't have long conversations in Waco, and for him, it was stimulating to be talking soulfully with his relatives. For me it wasn't; although usually pretty sociable, I remained in a grim mood, and after I accomplished simple chores the following day, such as applying for renewal of my Croatian passport (with a sombre portrait), I jumped into the Skoda and drove to Budapest. No one here comes out alive, the Doors lyrics ran though my head several times. I didn't see the old woman selling mushrooms. Maybe she grew tired too and went home to die.

I stepped out into the woods; after the a windstorm the night before, the sky became clear once again, even clearer than before, the visibility fantastic, the sun shining through beech and oak balding splendor of yellow and rusty red, while the wind shushed and whispered. He who has ears to hear, let him hear. I should write more in that vein of beautiful images and sounds but what could I say, I listened little and talked less. I had two lips and only one good unplugged ear. The other was still plugged from the airplane and cold.

While standing among the trees and looking up at them swaying and shushing, I wondered, why am I doing this, already writing about her and her life and death in my head. Would I finish it and put it on paper in Pennsylvania? Couldn't I write something else?

Near Budapest I found the rental agency easily and returned the car. The clerks credited back the $20,000, and ran the card again so I would pay 210 euros, the weekly rate. They walked around the car, complained about a scratch, but then waved and went back to their kiosk. Their assistant gave me a ride to the airport, and there I got a cab to the centre of the city where I rented a hotel room. It was near the Fish Castle. I walked down to the other side of the Danube to Pest and listened to gypsy music in a nearly desolate restaurant. The violinist came to me and played into my plugged ear. I loved the melodies slowing down, breaking down harmonies and keys, as though to say, the world is out of whack, it's falling out of its orbit and straying, and it's no longer turning on its axis. Of course, I tipped the musician for his wonderfully disorienting sounds and that encouraged him so he played more and wanted to sell me his CDs. His hair was oiled and you could see where he'd run a comb through it. I thought of my great-grandfather Josip who had been killed by an oak he had felled as a lumberjack, when my grandfather Josip was three years old, in southern Hungary. They had all spoken Hungarian, and great-grandmother was a Hungarian, Nemeth.

I walked in the streets. Vacy Street, cobbled and fashionable, worked as a promenade. Several pretty women exchanged glances with me, and I reminded myself, Not now, even though it would've been perhaps an absorbing distraction to chat with one of them. Three of them stopped me. I wondered whether they had sensed my gloom; I had walked in the street before, and none had stopped me then. They offered their services, and I laughed when it turned out that the better the woman looked, the less she would charge. No, thank you, *Kussenem sepem.* I had emailed Tibor Fischer, my writer friend, who was usually in Budapest when I visited London, and now he was in London, so there was nobody for me to visit. Strange—I had spent so much time in Budapest but that was before the Internet, and I'd lost touch. The few people I could still see lived in different towns. No matter. I was decompressing from the funeral, and my feet, now in sneakers, enjoyed walking after being crunched in the stiff black shoes. I walked to the hotel up the hill after having two cold beers in a pub, where a young bartender and his fake-blond girlfriend eagerly talked with me to practice their English and find out whether they could study at an American university. I told them America was over, done. Best to avoid America. But you are going there, they said. Well, yes, I live there. I don't plan to die there. I'll move to Canada rather than die in the States, or I will go to Croatia and drown in the Adriatic. Our conversation dwindled after my lack of American patriotism had come out. When I stepped out into the street, it was unusually warm and I was sweating. Maybe it was good exercise to climb up the Fish Castle. No, it wasn't. By the time I got to the hotel I sneezed and coughed and then shivered all night long.

Images from the funeral kept coming back to me: the cold forehead of my dead mother, the wet and cold green soil streaked with earthworm holes, the sounds of the fistfuls of soil hitting the wood, the bees landing on the red and purple carnations.

The feel of the cold rubbery forehead skin of my mother chilled me, and so did the sleeplessness, and for one reason or another, I got a Fall bout of bronchitis, for the first time in thirty years. The childhood home, and my mother, who warned me about lung diseases constantly ... I don't know exactly what induced the cough, but while coughing, I had a sensation that I was doing it in my childhood's remembrance, and even more, in my mother's remembrance. The cough seemed to me a form of prayer and penance, and it actually made me feel less guilty about being a prodigal émigré son. And I sensed relief, that I was no longer a son. I could no longer disappoint parents by dying before them, and nobody else's opinion would matter, other than the opinions of my lungs, in which the ghosts and spirits of my forefathers and foremothers wheezed.

ACKNOWLEDGEMENTS

"Apple" appeared in *Ploughshares Discovery Issue* in 1988, and won the Cohen Award for the short story. "Be Patient" first appeared in *Narrative Magazine* in October 2008. "Ruth's Death" first appeared in *Boulevard Magazine*, in May 2007, and was listed as a distinguished essay in *Best American Essays 2007*.